LISA PHILLIPS

USA TODAY BESTSELLING AUTHOR

DESOLATION POINT

1

"I need your help."

Deputy Sheriff Ellie Maxwell shook her head and continued her trudge up the hill. Wasn't talking to yourself the first sign of madness? She sure felt crazy being out here after midnight.

Her flashlight bobbed with each step. The narrow path had an incline not quite steep enough to be unmanageable. Tough going in daylight, right now she had to keep her gaze on the dirt in front of her while her mind swirled with the details of this case.

No, it wasn't a case.

Yet.

She needed Drew's help, that was a fact. How else could she appeal to his nature? That small town, protect-the-little-guy thing in him would surely mean he jumped to help her. Right?

Ellie said, "I *need* you," to the night.

No, that wasn't better. In fact, it was probably worse. There was no way she could say that to Drew. Not now and not back when she was fifteen, when he'd been the untouchable bad boy in junior year. The guy she'd wished said, "Hi" to her in the hallway. But, of course, Drew never did.

She could do this by herself.

Maybe.

It would be hard to keep the sheriff in the dark when he'd already told her to drop it. She couldn't let it go, though. Not when she would always wonder what there was to find. She didn't want to ask Drew for help, but she had to.

People were being pressured to sell their homes when they didn't want to. Bribed, coerced and roughed up until they signed their property over. Or the bank made it look like they'd been foreclosed on. One guy had been laid off for no good reason and more than one family had found themselves in financial hardship. Forced to leave town. Businesses closing down, while the neighboring one flourished.

By themselves, it just looked like life in a small town. Altogether, it was a pattern.

Someone was controlling the town.

Ellie's boot snagged a clump of dirt and she stumbled. Normally she loved hiking this trail, part of the state park just outside of town. Three miles long, from the parking lot on the side of Highway 23 to Lookout Point. The view of the valley from up there was amazing. Well worth the six-mile round trip.

Tonight the ground was hard with frost, and the low clouds worried her enough maybe she should've checked the weather report. Was it going to snow? Hopefully not before she was back at home with hot chocolate and her favorite blanket pretending she didn't have an investigation to look into. She had the second shift tomorrow, and she was looking forward to sleeping in.

Some instinct she'd honed through years of being a deputy flared to life. Her torso shifted, halting her stride before she even realized part of her had registered...something. What?

Ellie glanced around.

An animal in the woods? There weren't any other people out here tonight. Just her, and the man she needed to speak with. She'd have called on him at home, but she didn't actually know where he lived. Which, considering her position with the sheriff's department, was frankly kind of disturbing.

Still, she knew Drew would be out here tonight, on the anniversary of his father's death. At the place where his father had shot himself, and then jumped off Lookout Point to end it all, broken at the bottom of the cliff. She didn't want to stomp on his grief with her own problems, but she needed to talk to him somewhere no one would see or hear them. They could set a time to meet later for coffee, when she'd explained the problem, and then she could lay out all the particulars.

A twig cracked somewhere to her left, maybe a hundred feet out. Ellie stayed still. While her senses assessed the world around her for some sign of danger, her mind went over— again—all the reasons why she shouldn't be out here.

How else was she going to track him down?

She had to do this.

She listened as she walked on. Headed for the lookout at the end of the trail. The lone figure sat on a rock, something in his hand. Like a paper. The moon was behind the clouds, but it wasn't pitch black. There was enough light to see.

A horse shifted, taking a side step.

Ellie smiled as she glanced over. *Winter.* No, he'd gotten that horse before sixth grade. This had to be Spring, Winter's daughter.

She heard the unmistakable slide of a gun being pulled from its holster. "It's Deputy Maxwell." A flashlight clicked on, destroying what night vision her eyes had achieved. Ellie put her hand up like a visor. "Lower that, will you?" She wanted to wince, not meaning to sound that snappy.

"I could've shot you." His voice rang out.

"I didn't mean to startle you." The flashlight lowered and then bobbed while he stuffed whatever had been in his hand into his jacket pocket. "I need to talk to you, though."

That feeling intensified. The horse shifted again, then shook its head. Drew Turner crossed the expanse of the clearing and stroked the animal's neck. "Easy."

Even watching them didn't rid her of whatever caused the hair on the back of her neck to itch. She shifted her shoulders under the padded jacket she wore. Her hands were cold even inside her gloves. The only reason her feet weren't cold was because she wore two pairs of socks inside the boots her dad had bought her for Christmas.

As the former sheriff, her father knew how to keep warm during long shifts.

"You're a hard man to find."

"Apparently not that hard." He glanced at the tree line beside the trail. A curl of hair peeked out from under his knit cap.

"I need a minute of your time. I promise it won't take long."

Drew glanced back. "Quick would be good." He still held his gun loose in one hand, while the other continued stroking Spring. Because she was nervous…or he was?

"I'm happy to pay your usual rates." It wasn't like the town could provide much work for a private investigator, right? There couldn't be that many people who wanted evidence that their spouses were cheating on them. Besides, he didn't even rent an office in town. A thought struck her then. What if he was homeless? "Or more, if you want."

"You can't afford me."

"You don't even know what the job is."

"I have enough going on right now."

Ellie thought back to the look on Sheila's face when she and Brad had been escorted…no, *evicted* from their property. Ellie had been there as the deputy sheriff, to make sure the former residents obeyed the eviction notice and went peacefully—without destroying any of the property. Except Brad and Sheila had lived on that land for twelve years. They hadn't been able to have kids. The land had been their legacy.

And now they were gone from the town they called home.

But not after Sheila had made that passionate plea to Ellie. *Don't let them do this to anyone else.*

Ellie needed Drew to look into this case—and any others like it—while she pretended like nothing was going on. The sheriff had advised her to let it go. Like Sheila's words were nothing but the ramblings of a bitter person. Or so he'd assumed. And the woman had only been trying to manipulate Ellie's feelings.

Don't let them do this to anyone else.

She'd tried to find out why they were evicted, but on paper it appeared above board. They simply hadn't paid their mortgage. Was that really what had happened? Why had Sheila looked so scared? Why had her husband looked to have recently been in a vicious fight? It also begged the question why Ellie cared so much about them when she barely managed to care about herself most days. She didn't need to feel for the people she met through her job. If she felt this strongly for everyone she dealt with, she'd be overwhelmed by the pain.

Instead, she kept a lid on *any* feelings. Too scared she would be dragged under the swell of her own pain. Drowned by the undertow.

Drew took two steps and swung up on his horse. "Don't stay out here too long. It's gonna snow."

"I need to talk to you."

"I have to get Spring tucked in for the night."

The care in his voice made her heart hitch. She steeled herself against it. "Then can you meet me for coffee, or something?"

"In town? Like, where people will see us?"

"What's that supposed to mean?"

"Like you don't know? A deputy sheriff can hardly afford to be seen in public with someone like me." He paused. "Until you need my help, that is."

He tugged on the reins and the horse shifted to the right. He was just going to leave her out here? It was almost eleven at night. What kind of gentleman did that? Especially when every instinct told her it wasn't safe out here. Didn't he feel that?

"I can offer you something else," she said. "If you don't want money, what about information? Surely you can use a contact with access like mine. Information I can pass your way that will help you with cases." So that wasn't legal, but maybe it would get her his cooperation. She could figure out the particulars of the arrangement later.

His teeth flashed, white in the darkness, and he actually laughed. "You know nothing about the kind of man I am, Eleanor. I could turn you in to the sheriff just for that."

Everyone called her Ellie, but her Mom had named her Eleanor. Just hearing it out loud stung. "Don't call me Eleanor." Her temper flared, warming her from the inside. "I thought you might like to do something good for this county. Maybe help some people. I guess I was wrong."

"I've got stuff going on."

Whatever that was, she didn't care.

A single gunshot rang out.

The short scream escaped her mouth before she could pull it back. Her knee hit the frozen dirt, and she let out another cry. Head ducked. Pain sparking up her shin bone. She pulled her gun and scanned for the shooter even while she tried to figure out where to go. She needed cover. But she would also get shot if she made a run for it. Bullets were faster than she was.

More gunshots sounded. A hunting rifle, but this was no sportsman.

"Come on!"

The horse came close. She heard the animal before she saw it and scrambled out of the way. Drew's gloved hand appeared in front of her face.

"Get on."

———

SHE SLAPPED her hand up against his forearm. They clasped wrists, and he pulled her up. Eleanor climbed on behind him and slid her arms around his waist. He kicked Spring with his heels.

The horse shot between two trees, headed for home. Spring knew the way between here and his cabin well enough he hardly needed to direct her. But he kept a good hold on the reins anyway. His way of saying, "I'm here with you." The only thing that worked. That helped his horse keep her cool while bullets flew.

The worst time for a horse to freak was the second he needed her to help him keep *his* cool.

Eleanor's arms tightened around his bulky jacket. The deputy sheriff was stronger than she looked. Not that he'd been looking…except that one time she'd been choosing tomatoes in the grocery store. Her indecisiveness had been cute then. Now she was back to annoying him like the rest of the local law officers.

Drew thought he remembered her from high school. He had this one particular memory he thought for sure was her, but couldn't be sure. Most of the time, he tried to forget that time of his life. The same way he tried to keep a good distance between himself and the county's finest. It made for a much more solid state of mind when he didn't have to pretend they were doing a good job.

Thankfully the rifle fire had stopped. Drew didn't let Spring slack off on her pace though. She would, too. The horse was lazy most of the time—which was why he had to bring her on long rides in the cold just to get her out of her comfort zone.

He blew out a breath, and it puffed white in the cold night air. He'd have to interrupt Spring's journey home to circle back to the parking lot where the deputy had probably left her vehicle. It would be warmer to head to his cabin and then drive her in his truck. After he dropped her off, he could go hunting.

Five minutes later, Spring began to slow. That momentary rush of energy was gone, and she was back to her usual unmotivated self. He wanted to smile but had to face the fact that this sheriff's deputy had almost been killed in front of him. It didn't sit right, regardless of who had been the target.

"Someone trying to kill you?"

"They aren't very good at it if they are."

That depended on the kind of equipment the person had access to. They probably would have hit her if they'd had a heat scope.

"Maybe they were trying to kill *you*."

Drew pressed his lips together. "Or trying to scare you. Or me."

"Maybe both of us."

"Maybe." He wasn't so sure about that. It wasn't like they knew each other. He hadn't known she would be there tonight, but she seemed to have known he would be. Nor had he known she would show up at the spot where his father had thrown himself off Lookout Point in order to commit suicide. How could anyone have known they'd both be there together?

That meant it was more likely that he had been the target.

She said, "I'm glad they didn't hit Spring."

"You know my horse's name?"

"Winter was her mother, right?"

"Uh-huh." How did she know that?

"She chewed through your fence that one time. Wandered into town. My dad found her eating the flowers at the church."

He remembered that. "That must have been fifteen years ago." Long enough he'd lived several lifetimes since then. Or at least it felt that way, when he had to force his aching body out of bed in the morning. He was pushing thirty, but only barely. Why did he feel so old most of the time?

Spring headed for the back of his cabin. Probably because the barn was where her feed box was located. He tugged on the reins before the open door and said, "Hop off, yeah?"

Eleanor did as he asked, and Drew took care of his horse. When he shut the barn door he found the deputy in the same spot, except she now had one foot out. Tapping the dirt. Working herself up to some kind of argument he wasn't going to like.

"Do you have an open case right now that might make someone target you?"

Not what he'd been expecting. "Right now, no."

"So you have in the past." She tipped her head to the

side. "Jealous husband?"

Was that all she thought he did? He'd been right, she really had no clue what his job entailed. She thought he was just a regular private investigator. Most people saw what they wanted to see. Thought what they wanted to think, too swayed by emotion to see the truth right in front of their faces.

"I'll get the keys to my truck. Take you back to your car."

Hopefully it would start tonight. He should've replaced it two years ago, but he'd had expenses then and was almost done saving for a new one now. One more contract and he would have enough to buy the vehicle he really wanted.

The deputy followed him around to the front door of his cabin. She stood peering inside while he retrieved his truck keys from the kitchen counter.

When he wandered back to her, she said, "Huh."

Did he really care that the inside of his house was not what she was expecting? Not really. Part of him might want to know what she had going on that she thought he could help with. Professional curiosity, he'd call it. The rest of him didn't want to have any time for someone who made judgments about people like that.

It'd been happening all his life.

He's the kid whose father killed himself.

Obviously didn't love him enough to stick around.

The bad kid.

The rough kid.

Those labels were hard to shake. Even he believed them sometimes—and that would be all the time if it weren't for the couple who'd taken him in. The job he'd found. The life he had made away from this town, where no one knew his reputation.

That time was enough to store him up for when he came home and had to face the side-looks and glances. He still wore a leather jacket, though the one he had now was different than the one he'd worn in high school. The motorcycle was on blocks in one corner of the barn.

The deputy gasped and brushed past him into the living room. Drew glanced at the ceiling, then flung the front door shut. What on earth was up with this woman? "I kinda thought you'd want to go."

"This is…it's a North picture." Her voice sounded breathy. "I've never seen this one. It's *beautiful.*" She glanced at him, a look of awe on her face. "My best friend runs this gift shop in town, and she sells North pictures. I have three of them in my house."

A smile tugged at his lips. He didn't want to soften at her appreciation of his artwork, a photo of Lookout Point where she'd found him just a short time ago. A reminder to not let one event in the past define him.

A place where they'd been shot at.

"Did you forget you could've died a minute ago?"

"I didn't know I'd end up here." She shot him a smile. "But it was worth it just to see this. How much did you pay for it?"

"Come on." Drew went back to the front door, where he waited for her to join him. "I'll drive you back to your car."

Then he could go figure out who'd been shooting at them. Her. Him. It wasn't a *them* and never would be. This woman wasn't going to look past what she thought she knew to see the truth.

None of them ever did.

She seemed to suddenly realize she was in his house. Acting like something other than what she was—a professional. A sheriff's deputy. She nodded. "Of course." Then glanced around awkwardly. Out the front window.

Her eyes flared.

"There's someone outside."

2

"Get away from the window."

He sounded exasperated.

Ellie was already moving. Why he was exasperated, she didn't know. She touched her shoulder to the wall beside the window and peered out. Gun drawn. She reached back and slid her cell phone out of her back pocket. "No signal."

"I know. That's the way I like it."

"So how do we call for help?"

He frowned at her, then moved to the hall, calling back, "We are the help, remember?"

"I am." Ellie pressed her lips together. He was a private investigator in a small town. She was the local law.

He reappeared, holding a rifle. "I'll be back in a sec."

"Hold up." But he was already headed for the back door. "We can work together. Flush this guy out."

He twisted the lock and pulled the back door open. "There's a landline in the kitchen. Call it in."

Then he was gone.

She wanted to run after him, but he was right. The first thing she needed to do was call for backup. She had only her personal weapon on her. She wasn't on duty, the sheriff himself was on shift tonight. He would get the call. Ellie didn't especially want to see the look on his face when he showed up and she had to tell him why she was with Drew. Or that shots had been fired because of *her*.

Could have been an animal she had seen outside. Though, that didn't account for the gunshots. Would that be the first thing he said, another attempt to explain away her ideas? She didn't want Drew to get in an altercation with whoever was outside, but it would validate the call she was about to make if he did find a shooter.

Ellie hung her head. She wanted to pray but that part of her life was as dry as the rest. Nothing but frozen dirt. Hard. Unfeeling.

The way she needed it to be.

She dialed the number.

"Malvern County Sheriff." After hours, calls were routed straight to the on-call cell phone.

"Yes, sir. It's me." Ellie didn't hesitate to explain the situation and give the sheriff her location.

Silence. It lasted a few seconds, and then he said, "Are you going—"

The living room window shattered, the sound of a gunshot going off like a firecracker. She ducked as instinct flared. "Shots fired."

She hung up.

Of course he would have figured out why she was talking to Drew. At least, he knew her well enough to know she didn't go on dates. The only reason she'd be meeting with a male—or anyone—this late at night was if it were about work. Maybe she could just tell him she'd gone for a walk.

Ellie headed out back, skirting the outside of the house to the front lawn. Most of it had been graveled. She stopped and silence greeted her.

A distinctly male grunt echoed in the quiet, then the sound of a struggle. She ran toward it, not wanting to think what someone like Drew was capable of doing. Okay, so she was making assumptions. But if he'd wanted to be a police officer, he could've been. Right? Instead he'd decided to color outside the lines as a private investigator.

What would he do now?

She found them rolling across the ground. A rifle had been dropped, or discarded. She picked it up and held it with one hand, her own weapon in the other.

The two men hit a tree.

He rose up and laid a vicious punch in Drew's gut, then started to climb to his feet. Drew doubled over, gasping. Ellie planted her left foot, swung her other leg around and kicked the guy in the head.

He fell to the ground.

"You okay?"

Drew nodded, sucking in breaths. He climbed to his feet and they hauled the unconscious man between them, back over to the cabin where they deposited him on the porch. Drew disappeared inside, then came back with a plastic zip tie which he used to secure the guy.

"Did you shoot out the window, or did he?" She motioned to it.

Drew winced. "I'm just glad it didn't hit *you*."

Way to not answer the question. She said, "I called the sheriff."

How long it would take him to get there, she didn't know. It was a big county and he could be on the other side of it. Responding to a call. Waiting for speeding vehicles on the highway. Taking a nap. Nights like these were always quiet.

Drew crouched to go through the man's pockets. Wallet. Phone. She lifted the wallet and looked at the guy's driver's license. "Warren Shade. He's a local, according to the address. You know him?"

Drew shook his head. "You?"

"I don't think so, but I'll run his name when I get back to the office. Find out who he is." She rifled through the wallet. "Apart from a guy who had a dentist appointment four months ago."

She could get a ride with the sheriff back to her car. Or he could just drop her in town and she could have Laney drive her to retrieve it tomorrow morning. Her best friend wouldn't mind, and Ellie could talk to her about that North photo Drew had in his living room.

She glanced at her watch and saw the sheriff pull into the drive out the corner of her eye. She lifted the same hand and waved so he knew where they were. In her other hand she still held the rifle. "This yours?"

Drew looked at the rifle, then her. "It's his. I'll have to grab mine."

"Why don't you do that now?"

He shot her a look, but she pretended it was too dark to see it. How could she know what it was supposed to mean? The same look he'd given her in the hallway freshman year, when he'd smiled and said, "hi" to her. It hadn't meant he wanted to know her. Far from it. She'd been practically invisible to him the rest of the time.

Since then she'd lived through the worst relationship ever —one that had ended in tragedy. Ellie wasn't going to let another person cause her that much pain. Not again.

The sheriff looked from Drew to her as he made his way over. No time to let her thoughts drift, even if she'd desperately wanted to distract herself.

Thankfully Drew was out of earshot when Burgess asked, "This the guy who couldn't hit you?" He waved at the unconscious man on the ground.

"I'm not sure who he was aiming at." She folded her arms. "But neither Drew nor I are hurt, if that's what you're asking."

Yes, she was being defensive. Was it her fault?

Maybe.

Still, he didn't need to dismiss every idea she had. Or never compliment her the way he did the two other deputies. He even bought their receptionist and dispatcher, Barbara, pastries. Ellie's father had been the sheriff before him, and so apparently that meant she wasn't deserving of basic respect.

She'd tried earning it, but he'd basically laughed at her attempts to make more effort. And yes, she was kind of whining about her job. But she'd had a bad night of getting shot at and then taking her frustration out on the guy whose help she needed—someone who could investigate this case outside of official channels.

"Wanna tell me why he has a knot on his head?"

"I kicked him."

"And you're certain he's the one who shot at you?" The sheriff straightened to his full height. Probably taking pleasure at the fact he could look down his nose at her. She didn't want to believe that was it. He said, "You told me you were over at Lookout Point. You really think he followed you all the way here just to try again?"

"I think someone doesn't want me looking into why Sheila and Brad were forced out of their home." It had to be connected. She didn't believe in coincidences and coming out here tonight had been about finding out what was happening in town.

"It was an eviction, Maxwell. That happens when you don't pay your mortgage."

Ellie pressed her lips together.

The look on his face wasn't good. Like she was unhinged, and he was thinking about taking her to a doctor.

Maybe he should. Sometimes she thought she might be going crazy.

———

BOTH OF THEIR bodies were tense. Waves of frustration Drew could almost see, even from this distance. He slung the rifle across his back, then flipped the strap so it lay flat on his shoulder.

Was the shooting about him? He'd certainly made enemies in his line of work, that couldn't be denied. It was the nature of taking undercover cases from the feds.

The scope of his career went far beyond the boundaries of this county, despite what Eleanor might think. Someone could have traced him here. Though he took steps to remain as below the radar as he could.

He lived in the cabin he'd grown up in—the one he went to after his father had jumped to his death—even though they kept his name off the lease. Having emotional ties at all was dangerous, but God had given him favor. This far. The house was in Alma and Eric's names, and they were enjoying life in a Florida retirement community. Drew visited them as often as he could.

He thanked God right then that this guy who'd shot at him and Ellie hadn't tried the same thing down south. Alma and Eric might have gotten hurt.

If things changed here and someone had come seeking vengeance for something, he would find out soon enough.

He couldn't help wonder about the paper in his pocket. Did this have to do with the letter he'd found in his father's things? Yet more proof that nothing good came from being nostalgic. He'd found the box while he'd been clearing out his storage unit. A bunch of his father's old stuff. A pair of boots, a hat. Papers. A photo album full of grainy black and white images of men in uniform…and one wedding photo.

Drew gritted his teeth but didn't want to think about the woman his father had been hung up on. Though if she hadn't died, then his dad wouldn't have knocked up someone else. That woman hadn't stayed either. She'd chosen to leave Drew and his father.

But the grass wasn't greener somewhere else. Anyone who thought that was kidding themselves because they couldn't see the good to be found right where you were. If you had no contentment, then you couldn't have peace or joy. Or real love. Or a home to call your own.

That was how he knew Alma and Eric had saved him. They'd lived out God's love in his life, passing on that gift of belonging. Finding peace and contentment. He'd taken all that on board when he accepted Christ into his life.

Drew headed for the deputy and her boss. Squared off against each other over the unconscious man. Drew had nearly cheered when she kicked the guy. And she hadn't even seen the knife he'd been about to kill Drew with.

What would he have done with it after he'd finished Drew? Would he have gone after her?

A shudder ran through Drew that had nothing to do with the cold.

"…don't recommend that you put too much stock in this PI. It's not like he has much of a business in town," the sheriff was saying. "He's not going to find anything."

Drew held his breath, waiting for Eleanor's reply. He didn't want to put that much value in what she thought of him. He'd probably only be disappointed. Still, he did want to hear her answer.

"What if he does?" She sounded hopeful. "What if there's something to find?" Or, at least she was more concerned with her case than she was with how she felt about Drew…and his ability to investigate anything.

The sheriff didn't seem to agree with her. He lifted a gloved hand to scratch at his chin. "It's unlikely. You'll see that if you think about it. What happened to Brad and Sheila, losing their house like that after everything they've been through? It's a tragedy, that's for sure. But it couldn't be helped. They must have gotten behind on their mortgage. Far enough they couldn't make it up. You don't have all the details."

"Then I'll find them. I'll find out what happened."

"Nothing happened. You aren't going to find anything other than folks hard up. Everyone is right now." The sheriff looked at his watch. "Dragging Turner into this won't solve anything. Especially when he's only going to try and dig up something that isn't there. You know how people are. They want to impress you because you are the sheriff's daughter."

She shifted. The hand she moved behind her back squeezed into a fist. Didn't like what her boss had to say?

That made two of them.

"He isn't like that." It sounded like she spoke through gritted teeth.

The sheriff shook his head, even though she was right. He spotted Drew walking over and lifted his chin. When Drew was close enough, he called out, "I'm going to take this guy in." He glanced at the deputy. "Statements, Ellie?"

"I'll get Drew's and come in on shift to do my paperwork."

"You're on at noon, right?"

She nodded. *Ellie.* He'd forgotten everyone called her that. Why did it suit her? Before Drew could figure it out, she said, "Yes, Sir." Her tone was clear. She wasn't happy, but she was going to be a professional.

The sheriff gave him a short nod. "Turner."

"Night."

He watched the sheriff lift the unconscious guy and walk away carrying him all by himself. Because he was too stubborn to ask for help? Drew looked to his front window and tried to figure out if he had boards he could use to cover it until he got new glass put in. Eric was going to be disappointed someone had damaged the house, but he wouldn't be mad. Drew wasn't sure he'd ever gotten angry about anything in his life.

For a grieving hot-headed kid accustomed to yelling, that had been the strangest thing.

Truth be told, he still wasn't exactly used to it.

Drew preferred action, not sitting around. Or even praying about everything, though he tried to do that as much as possible. He needed the peace it brought. The wisdom God wanted to give him, and did.

Enough he could let other people's comments wash over him. Not get twisted up and torn up by what other people thought.

"Give me what you've got," Drew told her. "I'll take a look at your case."

"What if it is nothing?" She sighed. "Maybe that guy was trying to kill you, not me." Or she'd been the target, and it had nothing to do with Brad and Sheila. Or Drew.

"I'd rather not take the chance." With her life. "So pass over your file first time you get the chance. I'll let you know if I find anything." And if he was looking, it meant she was out of the line of fire. He would draw that himself.

Outside of regular foreclosure, people didn't get forced out of their homes. Not for nefarious reasons. That wasn't something he even wanted to believe happened these days. Maybe in the old west. Nowadays there were regulations protecting people's rights. Greedy moguls might be everyone's favorite people to hate, but that didn't mean justice was forgotten.

The letter in his pocket sat heavy with the weight of emotions he didn't know how to name. Addressed to his father, it had been delivered two days before he'd killed himself.

An eviction notice.

The bank had sold his land, and the investor wanted him out in fourteen days.

"Thank you."

He nodded, his head full of thoughts. Years had passed. There was no way the two events were connected, otherwise it meant there was some long-running conspiracy happening. Or at least someone buying up land around town, forcing people out of their homes for their own gain. What investor? He could look into it.

Not for Ellie. For himself.

Someone would have noticed. There was no way the two events were connected. But if they were, Drew supposed his particular skills meant he was uniquely qualified to find out. And if there was something going on? He and *Ellie* could both be in danger.

Either way, Drew would find out.

3

Ellie waved to the barista and stepped outside. She took a sip of her Americano and slid on her sunglasses. Drew should be here any second. He'd left her a voicemail before her alarm had even gone off this morning.

Because he'd *already* found something.

"Hey." Drew stepped onto the sidewalk and headed her way. His truck was parked across the street. "You have a drink?"

Her eyes drifted from the manila envelope in his hand, to his face. "Did you want a latte or something?"

His brow crinkled for a second. "Never mind."

Ellie tried to figure out what just happened. Did he want to sit? Had he shown up thinking they were going to "get coffee together" while he told her what he'd uncovered? And why did she want to…now that she thought about it. Until this moment, it hadn't even occurred to her that this might be about more than just the case she asked for help with. How dense could she get?

Before his feelings could get any more hurt, she said,

"Sorry. I'm so tired, I didn't even think you might want one. I can wait."

He glanced left along the sidewalk where an old man wandered toward them. Across the street a young mother pushed a stroller, followed by two school-age kids with backpacks.

Did he think… "It's not that I'm ashamed to be seen with you or anything like that."

His gaze shifted back to hers, a challenge in those flared brown eyes. He really thought that?

"Let's go inside."

He moved and tugged the door open. "You shouldn't be on the street for long."

Ellie paused before she stepped inside. "I'm not going to get shot at on Main Street in broad daylight."

"No, you won't be." He shrugged and followed her in.

Sounded like he was going to make sure of that. "The shooter is in jail."

He walked to the counter.

"I'm a deputy sheriff. I know how to take care of myself." She moved her cup close to her lips while they waited. "Besides, how do we know that guy wasn't shooting at you?" She took a sip, not liking how those words tasted.

He shrugged and said, "Americano," to the barista.

The teen girl glanced at Ellie, then at Drew. "Popular choice today."

When he looked at Ellie, she shrugged.

"Any word from the sheriff about that guy he took in last night?"

"Not yet," she said. "My shift starts at noon, so I'll find out when I get there."

Drew took his coffee, and they sat down. He got right down to business, flipping open the file. "According to what I found last night—" He took a sip of coffee. "—the company who purchased Brad and Sheila Harrison's land from underneath them is called Northcorp Inland Holdings. Which is a subsidiary of another company, that's a subsidiary of another company, etcetera, etcetera. And the only place Northcorp has any accounts are in Belize."

"Tax haven." Ellie fingered the sleeve on her cup. "A shell company?"

"Looks that way."

She sighed, leaning back in her chair. "So it's a dead end."

"Not necessarily." He sat back in the chair and studied her for a full minute.

"You can trust me." Why she felt the need to tell him that, she wasn't all the way sure.

Maybe because she *wanted* him to trust her. Or she was just desperate to rid herself of that memory of the look in Sheila's eyes, and he was the first person who came along. The sheriff had told her not to look into it.

She'd known who Drew was for years. He kept a cool head in stressful situations—at least he had last night. Still, they didn't know each other. Not really. Not yet. It was almost like they were testing each other to get a feel for how this would go.

Would they end up friends? She wasn't after more—not with anyone. Too much water under that bridge. She'd lit a match and now the bridge was just ashes. The destruction her past had wrought in her life.

Ellie was going to do her job and make a difference in the lives of the people in this county, and it was going to be enough.

He seemed to come to some sort of decision, because he said, "Nothing I do is illegal. My job has put me in contact with…people who have security clearance."

"So you *do* have access to stuff I don't." She stared him down. "What is it?"

The barista brought over a steaming hot burrito. Drew unwrapped it and took a bite. "You already ate?"

She shook her head, a slight smile tugging at her lips. Didn't want to answer the question, or couldn't?

She said, "It isn't like I thought you were a criminal." Not like the sheriff had tried to imply to her last night. "I just couldn't figure out how you make a living in a small town like this. There can't be many big paying jobs."

"There aren't. I supplement my income in a few different ways, one of which is skip tracing."

Realization dawned. "You're a bounty hunter."

"Occasionally." He tipped his burrito in her direction. "Want some?"

"I don't eat breakfast."

"Ever?"

She shook her head, not wanting to get into that discussion. People always thought it was weird. So she said, "A bounty hunter," and sat back in her chair, studying him. "I can see that."

"What is that supposed to mean?"

"Come on." She felt her lips curl up. "That whole bad-boy thing you had going on in high school? That *totally* says, 'bounty hunter.'"

Drew chuckled. "Not sure that makes sense, but okay."

He finished his burrito and they stepped outside together, standing close for a second as she moved out the door. He held it again for her, of course. It was like a dance. One with steps she was unfamiliar with.

"Okay?"

He'd caught her in her thoughts. She said, "Where to?" Totally avoiding the question the same way he had done.

"The real estate office."

They set off in that direction. Waved to a few people. Ellie ignored the looks they got from an older couple who gave Drew a wide berth. Whatever. When they reached the storefront of her best friend's gift shop and bookstore, Ellie picked up her pace so Laney didn't see her. Usually she rapped on the glass of the window and waved.

She glanced inside to make sure her friend hadn't noticed them.

Laney looked over, a stack of books to be shelved in her hands. She grinned at Ellie, then saw Drew. Her reaction was like a tennis match in middle school. Look at him. Look at her. Giggle.

Great. Her phone was going to start buzzing a mile a minute in a second. Laney always wanted to know everything.

Even when her life was at its worst, Laney had dragged everything out of her. Ellie had tried to break up with her as well, ditching her best friend for the sweet solitude of being alone and in pain. Laney hadn't accepted.

Drew chuckled.

Ellie shifted to look at him. "What's that?"

"She's sweet."

Her foot caught and she stumbled forward.

"Are you okay?"

"Sure. You know Laney?" They continued walking.

Not that Ellie cared if Drew knew her friend. Much. Laney was in a relationship, though evidently it might end soon. She'd told Ellie that a couple of nights ago.

He shrugged. "Just as a shop owner for the most part."

Okay, so apparently she was wrong. There wasn't anything there.

Ellie glanced at her watch even though she didn't especially need to know what time it was. Why should she be so concerned with how Drew felt about her best friend? She should be satisfied he thought Laney was sweet, a business owner. She *was*. Both of those.

But the real issue was how Ellie felt about herself. It didn't take anyone long to agree that Laney really was sweet, as well as being completely gorgeous. Meanwhile Ellie had her hair pulled back in a ponytail ready for work. Minimal makeup. Her style was more about function than trying to attract attention to herself, which she knew wouldn't keep her from being hurt again.

But if they did get into a relationship—no thanks—then he'd eventually leave anyway. Or she would drive him away. It was how every relationship she'd ever had ended. And the last one had been the worst of all.

Ellie sighed. "Let's go."

———

HE HAD LISTENED to Laney speak about her best friend many times over the years. That was Ellie? He still remembered the time Laney told him that her own name was actually Elenor even though everyone called her "Laney," and that her best friend's name was Eleanor, too. Same name, two spellings. She'd literally written it down for him, as though it were pertinent information.

The knowledge that Ellie was the best friend Laney had been referring to slipped through his mind like several puzzle pieces clicking into place at once. Nothing that could be considered a betrayal of confidence. But he realized now that maybe he knew Ellie better than he'd thought.

Better than she knew.

There was no time to think on it, though. Not with all the stuff swirling around them right now.

She got to the real estate office first and pulled the door open herself. The bell jangled. The receptionist looked up from the open lid of the copier that was toward the back of the waiting area.

"Morning."

The woman blinked. "Good morning." Her straight blond hair shifted as she turned and sauntered to them, her attention on Drew.

He shifted and wandered away. Forward, toward a rack of flyers showing houses for sale. Ellie could take point with this. It had only cost him a second to assess this woman, and he didn't want to buy what he knew she would try to sell him.

"We're looking for Simon Mills," Ellie said, her voice all business. Did she flash the woman her sheriff's badge? "Is he here?"

"Uh." The woman stuttered. "You're with the sheriff's department." Yes, Ellie had shown her the badge. "He has an appointment this morning, but he'll be back after lunch."

"And your name?"

"Natalie." Her voice broke. "Natalie Benson."

Drew lifted a flyer for a forty-acre spread northwest of town. He'd driven out that way, and there was a nice view of the mountains.

Ellie said, "Here's my card. If you could have him call me when he gets in. I'll swing by."

"Of course." If there was any friendliness there, it was all for show. "I'm happy to."

Drew resisted the urge to snort. There was a woman in this room who seemed genuine, and it wasn't the receptionist for the real estate agency. Natalie Benson didn't like being questioned by a cop. She might know what Simon Mills was up to and be acting squirrely because of it. Or she had secrets of her own.

Then there was Ellie.

Drew had friends now, sure, but back in school no one had been that for him. The only peace he'd found was at home with Eric and Alma. He'd been the kid whose father committed suicide. Just that. Not someone to take the time to get to know, only pity. And certainly not someone to go to great lengths for—what Laney did for her friend.

Maybe he and Ellie were more similar than he'd first thought. Had she suffered a loss? He wanted to ask her, but it was probably better they kept this about her investigation. After all, her life was in danger. They didn't need to be friends. They needed to trust each other's professional skills more than find some footing on a personal level.

Keep it professional. That was the important thing, right?

Drew's phone rang in his pocket. He turned and saw Ellie glance over to him. He pulled out his phone, then opened the door. Cold air buffeted his face. Maybe she would get some information about Northcorp out of the receptionist while he was outside on the phone. Or maybe she wouldn't. But he knew she was going to stay in there and at least try.

He answered the phone. "Turner."

"I found something." Mark sounded distracted, not normal for the FBI Director. Mark Welvern had laser focus. "About that company you asked me to look into."

"Yeah?" He and Mark had worked a few federal contracts together, crossing paths to the point they'd become friends.

When Mark needed a particular skillset—or someone he trusted with no visible ties to law enforcement—he called Drew. This was one of the first times since they met that Drew had called him for something, instead of the other way around. Now Mark was finding information to help Drew with *his* investigation.

"After I got done trying to dig up something that wasn't there, I went after the accounts. Got a list of everyone with check writing authority on the account from the bank in Belize."

Drew's eyebrows rose. "How'd you get that?"

"I asked nicely."

"Right." Drew didn't believe it for one second, but the guy was a fed. Some people got one look at the badge and started talking.

"Fine," Mark said. "I phoned a friend who has a friend."

"Talia?" The woman was an NSA analyst and a member of the Northwest Counter-Terrorism Taskforce. If anyone could get information, it was her.

Drew had worked with them on a couple of cases. Victoria hadn't offered him a job but he figured that was because if she had asked, he wouldn't have taken it. He had no interest in a badge. Or a career that tied him down to a particular region, or a certain type of case.

"Fine, so you know all my friends," Mark said. "Do you want the information, or not?"

"Hit me."

"Your real estate agent there in town? His name is listed on the board of Northcorp Inland Holdings."

Drew paced the sidewalk. "Isn't that stuff public record?"

"Not the way you think, and not how they set this whole thing up. There's a website, I'm sending you a link, that's all we found. Other than this one guy, Simon Mills, we have no idea who is behind that company."

Drew watched a car drive past and turned back to the real estate office. "There's no one else?"

"No one who is actually a real person."

"Huh."

"Now you see my dilemma." Mark was quiet for a second. "Wanna tell me why you're suddenly interested in something homegrown instead of getting into everything you can that takes you out of town?"

"I'm not trying to escape." Where did Mark get that idea?

"Not like you can just move. What will Alma and Eric do with their house then?"

"Rent it out, like they do for me. Or sell it." Drew sidestepped for the mail lady, frowning at Mark's insinuation. He could leave whenever he wanted.

He'd been their only tenant since they retired to Florida and left the house to him. Drew had turned down their offer to gift him the house. He wanted it to remain in their names. In return, they kept the rent so low Drew often sent them extra money. Sure, they had retirement accounts, but he also knew they weren't flush. Who was these days?

"Sure," Mark said. "But you don't want to leave them in the lurch."

"Except you just argued that I *do* want to leave." Drew was super confused.

"It's called self-sabotage, duh."

"Have you been seeing the shrink again?" Drew shook his head. "You sure are getting some funny ideas."

Mark was quiet for a minute, then said, "I'm listening to this book while I run."

"You should probably switch back to music." Even though Drew did the same thing. He got all kinds of ideas from reading books. But he would admit, to himself at least, that he steered clear of books designed to dig up the past. Or analyze his feelings. Neither of those would help him move forward with his life.

"I still think I'm right."

"That I'm running from something but also not willing to go anywhere? That makes no sense, you know."

"I'm still right."

Drew hung up, ready to laugh. If he wasn't standing

alone on the sidewalk, maybe he would have. He would look like a crazy person if he started laughing to himself.

He scanned the street and the sidewalks on both sides, mostly out of habit. Situational awareness was key. Mostly due to the fact that, if he didn't maintain it, he'd have already been killed. Maybe not here, but certainly working one of those federal jobs.

His truck sat at an angle. Like…

Drew ran the three steps to the door and called for Ellie. When she spun around he said, "Someone slashed my tires."

4

"Did you know you parked your truck perfectly between the bank's ATM camera—" Ellie pointed to it, then shifted. "—and this traffic camera. Making it completely invisible."

He scratched at his jaw. Maybe he hadn't known that. He said, "You aren't saying this is my fault?"

She tapped her foot on the sidewalk. "No. I'm not." She looked at her watch. "Listen, I have to get to my shift. Can you call Frank to tow it, or you want me to?" She set off toward the sheriff's office across the grassy area.

"I can call for a tow." He stepped onto the crosswalk with her, heading for the moment in the same direction she was. The grassy area in front of the mayor's office was peppered with people—even a class full of kids enjoying a picnic. Field trip? The sheriff's office was the next building down from the mayor and his staff. The county court was a block over.

"Good idea." Ellie blew out a breath, mostly frustrated about the lack of progress she'd made with the receptionist, Natalie Benson. Never heard of Northcorp Inland Holdings. Didn't know how many properties they'd bought. What kind of person did what they were told without asking any questions? That was just weird.

"One second." Drew halted her with a hand on her arm before she could head across the path that cut through the grass. "I need to tell you about my call."

A minute later she glanced back at the real estate office, contemplating the knowledge that Simon Mills was so immersed in Northcorp Inland Holdings that he was actually listed as a board member. "Now I wish I'd known that before I went in there and talked to Natalie."

"Puts it all in a different light, knowing Simon Mills is behind the company buying up property all over town. And they've been doing it for years."

"What do you mean?"

He rifled in that manila envelope again. The one he'd been holding this whole time. "Here."

She looked at the paper he'd given her. "Northcorp Inland Holdings bought…oh."

"Right."

They'd bought his father's land a month after the man committed suicide. She lifted her gaze and tried to read him. "They've been doing deals for that long?"

"I guess so."

"Is the real estate agent even that old?"

A light dawned on his face. "If he isn't, then he can't have been part of it back then. And he's only been in town a few months, right?"

Ellie nodded and handed him the paper. "I really do have to get to work. My shift starts soon and I need to talk to the sheriff about the guy he took in last night."

"Lead the way."

She frowned. "You're coming?"

"I'll have to, if I want to make a report about my slashed tires."

Why hadn't she thought of that? Because she wasn't on duty right now, so it wasn't her job. That was the worst excuse ever.

Something about today, and Drew being here with her, was throwing her off. She was out of her element. And yeah, she hadn't slept all that well replaying through her mind getting shot at and then racing away with a man on horseback.

A strong man. One who made her feel safe.

Ellie didn't remember the last time she felt that way. Years. Maybe not since she'd been a child. The strong man part *and* the horse part. Which made her want to talk to her father.

She'd have to call him later. See how he was. "Ask him about this."

"What was that?" Drew glanced at her.

She blinked, realizing she'd spoken aloud. He'd jumped on the first snippet of a conversation, desperate to break the silence. Hopefully he wasn't one of those people who thought quiet was peaceful. That would be terrifying.

"My dad." She tried to resurrect her train of thought and coax it to move again. "I should ask him about this holding company and see if he knows anything. He was the sheriff here for three decades. If something was going on, surely he'd have heard about it."

Drew nodded. "Good idea."

"But I literally didn't even think about you needing to file a report about your tires." Before he could ask her why, she said, "I'm just...out of it. Off my game."

"Today, or lately in general?"

She thought for a moment. "Just today, really. But I don't want to explain it away with an excuse."

"Wrapped in the skin of a lie."

"Where did you hear that?" She wouldn't be lying

outright, but an excuse didn't tell the whole truth. It only tried to justify things.

He shrugged.

It was *her* father who said that. He was also the one who'd instilled in her the need to continually move forward. But how could she do that when she felt like she was stuck? So stuck that everything had begun to go bad. Was her mental state today just another symptom of her life being stagnant for too long?

It wasn't like she had the time to figure that out right now. Not when bullets were flying, and Drew's tires had been slashed. She needed to clock in, talk to the sheriff, and then get out on the streets. Find the real estate agent.

They climbed the steps to the sheriff's department second floor office. Ellie led the way. Inside, their receptionist waved, on a phone call.

"Yes, thank you." Barbara hung up. "Afternoon, Deputy."

"Barb."

Drew stopped at her desk and told her he needed to report a crime. Ellie flipped the latch on the hip-height gate at the center of the counter and let herself into the office. The two holding cells were empty.

She knocked on the frame beside the door to the sheriff's office.

"He isn't here."

She spun to see Coughlan standing behind her. "Will he be in?"

Coughlan shrugged, a file in his hands. He'd given up on the fight against male pattern baldness and now completely shaved off his thinning hair. Today a ball cap covered his shiny head, and he overcompensated for his lack of hair by working out like a crazy man. His muscles stretched the short sleeves of his shirt to bursting. Not a look Ellie had ever favored.

"What about the guy who was in holding? Warren Shade."

"Told me to cut him loose."

"He shot at me last night."

"Sheriff said you'd say that, so he told me to tell you that it wasn't him trying to kill you." Coughlan glanced at Drew, who was listening and not writing his report on the form Barbara had given him. "You guys got the wrong guy. But if it makes you feel better, the sheriff is going to fine him for hunting without a license."

Ellie pinched the bridge of her nose. That wasn't what had happened. "He *fought* Drew."

Coughlan turned away. Like she'd said nothing. "And you've got patrol."

Of course she did. Because if the sheriff showed back up at the office today, it was best for him that she be out driving around and responding to calls. She shook her head, vaguely convinced that these sarcastic thoughts might be the beginning of a serious mental problem.

Ellie didn't even sit. She poured black coffee into a travel mug she kept on her desk and got a set of keys for a sheriff's department vehicle. She'd parked her own car in the lot behind this building before she met Drew for coffee. "I'm out."

She walked back to the front desk. "You need a ride home, Drew?"

"Actually to the tire store."

She nodded. "Turns out it's on my way."

Drew's gaze softened. "Thanks."

"No problem."

It wasn't just because she wanted to spend more time with him. There was plenty of this mess they could continue talking about. Hopefully they'd be able to unravel it enough to figure out what on earth was happening, because she felt like she was going crazy. Was there actually a corporation in town involved in a land grab?

Drew called Frank and had him tow the truck to the tire store while he finished filling out his report, and then they headed to the garage. Two miles into the three-mile journey, a truck pulled out from a side street doing sixty in a thirty-five.

"Sorry." She flipped on the lights and sirens.

"No worries," Drew said from the passenger seat. "You still need to do your job." Like that was something to be proud of.

It was, but she'd learned through experience that not many people agreed with that sentiment.

A quarter mile later she pulled to a stop behind the truck and glanced at Drew before opening her door. She had thought that she knew him, but maybe she had no idea who he was. What kind of man—and what kind of friend—he would be.

She really wanted to know.

———

DREW OPENED the email app on his phone and read through what Mark had sent him. Everything he'd been able to find on Northcorp Inland Holdings and the apparently fake names, with the exception of the real estate agent, listed all over the paperwork. Except for Simon Mills' name, the others were worthless. Mark had tracked them down as stolen identities.

Who was Simon Mills in all this? And how had he gotten involved in forcing people from their homes? Could be he was the mastermind, but not when he hadn't lived in town all that long. So who was behind it? How did this guy wind up listed on the company directory?

Soon as he got new tires and was mobile again, Drew was going to find out.

He glanced up and saw Ellie having a conversation through the window on the passenger side of the truck. Two men sat inside the cab. At least, he thought they were men. He might be wrong about that.

Her body language was stiff. Drew took a second to just observe. What was wrong; what was making her uncomfortable?

Ellie nodded, and he saw a smile. Maybe she was all right. Looked like she had enough of a handle on it. Or she was just a cautious cop, one with senses that had been affected last night in the woods. A situation like that would throw anyone off. He'd seen it happen with the feds he'd worked with, undercover agents who got shaken by something overwhelming. An event they couldn't control.

Drew pulled out his phone. He called Eric before he remembered it was Tuesday, and that meant he'd be playing golf.

"Hey there, son. How are ya?"

"Did I catch you at a bad time?"

"Nah," the old man said, a glint of humor in his voice. "I was losin' anyway."

Drew felt the pull of a smile on his lips. "How are you?"

"You really wanna hear about all that?" Before Drew could answer, Eric said, "Me and the old girl are fine."

"I'm glad to hear that."

"Still comin' down in a couple of weeks?"

"That's the plan." Drew tried to figure out how to ask the question in any other way than to just ask. So he said, "You ever hear of a company called Northcorp Inland Holdings?

Seems like they've been buying up property around town. Maybe for years."

Eric made a noise in his throat. One Drew had heard anytime the man was disappointed, or when he didn't want to talk about something. Which considering they'd taken in a grieving fifteen-year-old with a streak of wild running right through him, had been often.

But Eric and Alma had kept their promise. They'd supported him. They'd given him love, and a home. Neither of which he could've said he'd had before his father committed suicide. Not that his dad had been abusive. Plenty of people had it worse than Drew did for those fifteen years. But the home he'd found with Eric and Alma? Light years away from that dank nine-hundred square foot rundown cabin and the worn and smelly recliner his dad practically lived in.

"So you've heard of them." Drew let it hang out there, then he waited. Eric only ever did anything in his own time.

Considering Drew was equally as stubborn—and determined—had made for some interesting battles waged. Mostly over the fact Drew needed to make something of his life.

"Son." The word was long and slow.

"Whatever this is, it's too late to warn me off, Eric. They shot at me and Ellie last night." He still didn't know which of them had been the target, but he had a pretty good idea. "Today they slashed my tires."

"Ellie?"

Drew wasn't going to respond to the hopeful tone there. "Sheriff Maxwell's daughter."

"Caught their attention." Eric sighed. "Nothing good will come of this."

"What do you know?"

"Not much more than rumors. People being paid off,

pushed out of their land for one reason or another. Folks who lived 'round there for generations, suddenly pulling up stakes looking for a better life." Eric paused. "I didn't believe it."

"Neither do I." Drew ran a hand down his face. "I found an eviction notice. In my father's things." He'd never referred to him as "dad." Now Eric held that place in his life. He was the one who'd taught Drew how to be a man. Honest and hardworking. Someone who put the people he cared about first.

Drew didn't have anyone like that in his life except for Eric and Alma. No one else in town had ever taken the time to get to know him, gotten past what they all believed he was. He'd given up on finding a woman who would look at him the way Alma still looked at Eric, even after all these years. That wasn't the marriage most people had. He knew himself well enough to know it wasn't going to happen for him.

"He was losing his house?"

"The whole property had been sold by the bank and they wanted him out," Drew said. "Forty acres and the house. It was bought by Northcorp in another transaction that happened after he died." After the sheriff, Ellie's father, had dropped Drew and all his belongings off at Eric and Alma's.

He shook his head just remembering the way he'd treated them in those first few weeks.

"Hmm."

"They could've forced him out. Pressured him until he broke." And then he'd committed suicide, leaving Drew with no family.

Except the one God in His grace had given him.

Beauty coming from ashes. The kind of blessing that God was really good at.

"Can't say I heard anything like that, but we didn't run in the same circles."

Drew nodded to himself. "I know." The two men

couldn't have been more different. "Thanks for talking to me."

"Ah." Eric chuckled. It was amazing what he could convey through non-words. "Never a problem. You know that."

"Tell Alma I love her." He glanced up to see if Ellie was done with her traffic stop yet. She had one hand raised.

The driver walked around the vehicle toward her, while the passenger climbed out. There was nothing good about her body language now. Not one thing about the expression on her face or the way she stood, completely straight, made him want to remain in this truck.

She took a step back, arm still out straight. Hand, palm out, toward the men. A clear signal to stop.

One that neither man obeyed.

"Gotta go." Drew hung up and dropped the phone in the cup holder. What on earth were they—

The two men advanced on her, determined to crowd her backward. Ellie stood her ground, chin raised. Every bit the cop. She reached for her weapon.

Drew flung the door open. "Hey!"

One of the men swung around to see him. The other shifted his hand, and Drew saw the glint.

He had a knife.

5

Ellie reached for her weapon. The man lunged. His knife flashed as it reflected the sun overhead. She twisted as it came, then shoved at the man's wrist. The knife nicked her sleeve and she hissed.

Balled her fist and punched the man in the stomach.

He didn't go down.

To her left she could hear the staccato thuds of two people in a vicious fight. Drew and the other guy. He'd gotten out of her vehicle and come over to help.

So she wasn't outnumbered.

So she wasn't overpowered.

The man swung his arm again. His knife came back in for another swipe. No training, just a guy looking to make someone bleed. Little more than a hacking motion, his awkwardness suddenly stuck out to her, but she was forced to push aside the thought and make another move to defend herself.

She stepped back.

The knife sliced the air between them.

Ellie swung off her jacket. Cold air hit the back of her

sheriff's department tan shirt, but she ignored it and flung the coat in a swirl to make it wrap around her hand and arm. It would do double-duty; protect her from getting cut and at the same time, if she could time it right, cover the blade.

She swung it at the knife hand and got it around the blade.

Ellie grabbed the man's arm with her other hand, twisted her body so her back was to Drew and the other man, and kicked out. Her driving kick planted in the man's sternum.

He tried to grab her foot, his other hand incapacitated. She hopped a couple of steps and then used her left fist to punch. Not as powerful as her right, but it successfully dazed him. She really wanted to head butt the guy. Bad idea though, considering it would hurt her as much as it would hurt him.

Ellie said, "Drop the knife."

She kicked his legs out from under him, rolled him to his stomach and grabbed his free hand. She twisted it up his back and said again, "Let go of the knife."

It shifted in his grip, so she moved the coat out of the way. Then she grabbed and tossed the knife, pulled cuffs from her belt, and secured the man's hand. Finally, she could pull her gun out.

A thud to her left brought her attention around. Drew had his guy on his face, one knee in the man's back.

He pulled the guy's arms back in a move curiously similar to what she had just done. Holding the wrists, he glanced at her. "Cuffs?"

"There's a second pair in the truck. Keep an eye on this one, and I'll get them." She motioned to the man on the ground before her.

At the truck, Ellie called in and updated Barbara on what was going on. She left the anger out of her voice, though. Too many locals had police scanners. This would be all over

Malvern County before tomorrow morning, and she extremely disliked being famous.

Ellie tossed Drew the second pair of cuffs. She realized this was probably what it felt like to have a partner, like one of those city cops. Malvern didn't have the money for them to ride out in pairs after their training was over. The department was made up of only two deputies and a sheriff. They went together when they knew they'd need backup—like a takedown, or serving a search warrant.

Drew stepped back and hauled the other guy to his feet, then turned him toward her vehicle.

Ellie had a thought. "Hold up a second."

Drew shoved the man against the side panel of the truck bed. Both he and the man they'd secured turned their heads to look at her. Ellie yanked her guy up. "Let's go."

She walked him to stand beside his friend, then pulled the wallets out of their back pockets. Read their names aloud.

"Shouldn't we be taking them in?" Not a straight question from Drew, more like he was feeling her out. Seeing what her intention was here. Letting the two guys know she was in charge, and they were going to jail no matter what happened.

Frustration burned in her. The bleed off of adrenaline left her breath coming fast enough she had to work to slow it down. There was also a distinct sting on the outside of her arm. She'd been cut?

Ellie pushed that aside and said, "We will soon enough."

She needed answers before the sheriff just cut them loose with a slap on the wrist. *Maybe he won't get the chance to do that this time.*

If the sheriff had actually been at the office that morning, she'd have been able to talk all this out with him.

Convince him there was something going on here. Instead, it seemed like he was doing his best to avoid her right now.

"Okay then." Drew turned to the two men. "Start talking."

The guy in front of Ellie said, "My favorite color is yellow."

The friend snickered.

"You just assaulted a sheriff's deputy with a deadly weapon." Ellie paused. "Why?"

"Seemed like a good idea at the time," yellow man said.

"And when I find out your friend here—" She motioned to the guy in front of Drew. "—has two strikes against him already, what then? Both of you go to jail for a long time. No more truck. No more good times."

The muscle in his jaw twitched.

"Bet your girl wouldn't like that much." Just a guess, but it usually worked. While he thought about that, she studied the other one. Tried to figure out which of them was the alpha and which was just along for the ride.

Drew said, "Talk."

"We were paid." Yellow man made a face. "Hundred bucks to get your attention."

"And then?"

"Have some fun. Whatever. Didn't matter." His eyes darkened.

Drew said, "So you brought a knife to the party? Because you enjoy going to jail?" It was pretty clear he thought the whole thing was a bad idea.

Ellie kind of wanted to know if he was indignant on her behalf, because he didn't like the idea of her getting hurt, or if he just didn't like that these guys were dumb?

She said, "Who paid you?"

Her guy said, "Some guy at O'Doul's."

"You don't know who he was, just walked up to you at a bar, gave you cash and told you to commit a felony?"

When neither said anything, Drew asked, "Was it the real estate agent?"

The man in front of him frowned. Shook his head. "I'd never seen the guy before. Don't know who he was, and he didn't exactly show me ID."

Great. "So I can go ask the bartender if I can take a look at his tapes, get the man's picture? ID him that way? Then you can all be named in these charges and everyone will know you told us who hired you."

"Come on," the guy in front of Drew shifted and looked at his dusty boots.

"Not fair?" she asked. "Like it's not fair that I pull you over for driving crazy and you cut me? That kind of not fair?"

He made a face. Drew's head whipped around, as though he needed to assess the veracity of her statement—or the damage done to her with the knife. Or both. But she couldn't let that distract her. Care had no place here, and he wasn't her partner despite how it felt to do this together with him instead of alone for once.

She tugged her attacker away from the truck and walked him to her sheriff's department vehicle. "Let's go."

———

DREW WIPED his napkin on his mouth. "So what's the plan for later?"

He'd been trying to draw her out of her funk since they'd taken those two guys into the sheriff's office. They were on the west end of town now. Close enough to the garage that he could walk over and pick up his car in…he checked his watch. Half an hour to go.

Ellie swallowed a bite of the chicken sandwich she'd ordered for her dinner break. "I'll go back to the office. Maybe the bartender has sent me those surveillance tapes by now. I can also see what else I can find out about the people who've moved away from here in the last few years. And I'll try to locate the real estate agent. Simon needs to answer some questions about his business antics."

And what those antics might have to do with everything that'd happened since Ellie walked up to him at Lookout Point.

Not something either of them said, but it hung between them nonetheless.

She still had a few hours left on her shift, and he wanted to go out to the property his father had owned before his death. See what was there now that it was owned by Northcorp Inland Holdings. What could have possibly been worth forcing Drew's father out of his home…and to his death?

"This is for when you're ready." The waitress laid the pleather book containing the check and a cheap pen between them. "No rush." She wandered off.

Drew grabbed it before Ellie could, her hand two inches from doing the same thing. "I got it."

She eyed him.

"Because I'm nice like that." This wasn't a date. After all, he had better taste than the town diner—though their finger steaks were good. If this were a date, he'd have taken her to the steakhouse one town over. "Just a normal, everyday nice guy."

She cracked a smile, then took a sip of her drink. "I believe you."

He'd succeeded with that much at least. Enough he saw her let that dark cloud of whatever had been hanging over her slide off for just a moment. He felt the smile curl up his lips. "Of course you do. Because you'd never make a face-value judgment about someone."

Not like the rest of them.

"Maybe I should." She shrugged. "Then I'd have known earlier that those two guys intended…whatever it was they planned to do with that knife."

He didn't even want to think about that. About what would've happened if he hadn't been there? Would she be dead?

Or she might have wished she was.

He had no idea what they'd had planned to "get her attention."

Then he had to remind himself who she was. The fact she'd had a gun on her, though she hadn't felt the need to use it. "You took him down. A guy came at you with a knife, and you defended yourself."

"I got cut." She motioned to the torn sleeve, under which was a bandaged slice that she'd decided wasn't going to stop her from finishing her shift. It was barely an inch long, and not deep. Small enough she'd patched it up with stuff from the first aid kit in the bathroom at the office.

Drew shook his head. "If I hadn't been there, you'd have pulled your gun earlier right?" He had no problem with the idea she might have needed to shoot one of them in order to defend herself.

She sighed.

"Ellie." When she lifted her gaze, he said, "You're a good cop."

"I was scared."

"That's *why* you're a good cop. The ones who aren't scared are either lying to themselves, or worse. They make reckless decisions and the fallout from that is far more devastating. To innocent people and to their own careers."

"And how is it that you know this?"

He fingered his empty iced tea glass. "I take federal contracts. I have friends who are agents with the FBI, DEA. Even the US Marshals."

"Federal contracts?"

He nodded. "When they need someone to go in, get information for them. Someone whose identity is clean."

"Ever want to be one of them?"

"No." He shook his head. "I don't fit with the culture." The phrase, "doesn't play well with others" came to mind. Like that was a bad thing.

She cracked a smile. "I thought you were supposed to be convincing me you *aren't* still the high school bad boy who drove his motorcycle into the mayor's pool."

He chuckled aloud. "That story. It flew around so fast that by the time it got back to me I thought they were all talking about something completely different. That had nothing to do with me."

"Hot topic."

He hadn't wanted to be talking about history—though they shared a good amount if he thought about it. And if it put this smile on her face? He would do it. "Honestly, I have no idea why."

"Um." She let out a chuckle herself, one that smoothed out the lines of pain on her face. "Because you were the best looking guy in high school? I believe one of my friends even described you as not 'hot' but so hot that you were *hawt*."

He laughed. "I'm not sure I want to know about that."

"Deny it all you want," she said. "But you had enough girlfriends back then it can't have escaped your knowledge."

"Yet more stories that ended up out of hand." He took a sip. "There were a couple of girls who just wanted a ride on my motorcycle. Aside from that..." He shrugged.

"Really?"

He nodded, eyeing her. "People said what they wanted.

Never mind the truth." What he'd like to know was how she felt about him back then. "And then there was you."

Her eyebrows rose. "What about me?"

"The untouchable sheriff's daughter."

"Is that better, or worse, than being the preacher's kid?"

"I don't know," he said. "But I could visit the county jail and ask him if you want."

"Don't mention my name." She widened her eyes at his mention of the preacher's kid. "I'm the one who arrested him."

"I didn't know that." He wondered at it now. "High school feels like a million years ago. We're all totally different people."

"I am." She studied him. "But…maybe not so much you."

He waited.

"Maybe you're who you always were, but this is the first time I've noticed."

Drew took a sip, thinking that over. *Who you always were.* "A hot-headed punk?"

"Or not."

He shook his head. "You might be right about that."

Considering he did his best thinking in his truck, she had him at a disadvantage right now. He needed time to think this through. Both what she'd said, and that it was her who said it. Truth be told, he'd always known who she was. But, like he said, she'd been untouchable.

Especially for the kid he'd been—a hot-headed, motorcy-cle-riding teen boy. Talk about a recipe for disaster. It was a wonder he hadn't killed himself.

Alma and Eric had helped him figure out how to settle. Then they'd introduced him to Eric's brother, Uncle Merrick. The skip tracer. It had been the perfect outlet for his more risk-taking tendencies. Not to mention gainful employment right out of high school.

"For the record," he said, "the motorcycle never went *into* the mayor's pool."

She laughed. "I should get back to work."

"Be careful."

Her expression sobered and she nodded. "I will."

"I'm going to head out to the property my father owned. Talk to the current homeowners and see if they know anything."

She nodded. "Good idea. I'll patrol over there and come with you to take a look."

Maybe she was as reluctant for them to split up as he was. Every minute or so the mental image of her getting cut with that knife replayed through his brain. Never mind that he hadn't even seen it happen. His brain managed to come up with the image anyway.

Drew said, "We can meet there." As he walked over to get his truck, which had brand new tires now.

Once he got on the road he felt better. Halfway there he spotted her behind him and slowed a little so she could catch up. They pulled onto the forty-acre property together. Drew pulled up to a stop in front of the wreckage of the house he had lived in the first part of his life.

A house that should have been torn down and built over with something new years ago, at least according to the county assessor's records.

What was going on here?

6

Ellie slammed the door to her department vehicle and stared. From across the hood of his truck, Drew said, "That was my house."

Broken windows. The roof had caved in, and the whole right side of the house had collapsed under the weight of a tree that had fallen over. Debris from some storm. The roots of the tree had long since withered. Maybe that big storm they had six years ago?

Had no one come up here in all that time?

She crossed what would've been the yard. Close enough she could see water on the floor inside the open door. Wood splintered around the handle, the door lay askew. Floorboards inside were missing.

A cold breeze whipped through the trees. Ellie pulled out her gloves and tugged them on. The drive over had given her some time to think, but not nearly enough. She'd come up with nothing at the office before they headed out here.

She needed another shot at digging up information on the whereabouts of people who had moved away recently, and suddenly. Few of them had come up on any of her searches. The one man she'd managed to track down, she'd called and left a message. Then there was the police report she'd found—and a death certificate—for a woman who'd been killed in a car accident two weeks after signing on the sale of her house.

Ellie pulled out her phone and went onto the county assessor's website. She typed in the address. It listed the current homeowner, Rupert Smithson. One of the North-corp Inland Holdings board members—a stolen identity. The assessed value of the house that should have been standing on this property was close to three hundred thou-sand, a mid-sized family house in this area.

She glanced around, scanning the area. Forty acres plus the house.

But there was no house here. Just the dilapidated ruins of something that once resembled a house.

"What on earth is going on?"

"That's what I was thinking." He stood about six feet away, to her right. Beyond arm's reach if she was inclined to move her injured arm. Which she wasn't.

"Want to look around?"

He winced. "We'd probably just end up falling through the floor or something."

Ellie circled the outside of the house. More of a cabin really, or at least it had been at one time. Back when his father was alive, and Drew had lived here. She remembered him even from those days before his father died. He'd had that streak of wild in him back then. Now she knew kids like that. Ran into them on her shifts. Caught with spray paint, tagging someone's barn. Stealing candy bars or sodas from the store in town.

Couple of them she even checked on every few weeks,

just to make sure they were sticking to the promise they'd made her to clean up their lives.

Because they reminded her of the boy Drew had been? Maybe.

He met up with her at the back side of the cabin. "Anything?"

She glanced at the wreckage. "Sure you don't want to go inside?"

"What's there to see? There should be a new house here, and there isn't. This was supposed to have been torn down years ago, but it wasn't."

"It's a pretty big property. We should walk through it." She was on shift, so she couldn't do that right now. But it would be prudent to check all of the forty acres and make sure there wasn't something here they were missing.

"We can."

"Maybe tomorrow morning? I don't have a shift." She would have to call Laney and let her know she couldn't help out in the store tomorrow, but she could make it work.

He nodded, his gaze distant as though his thoughts were far away. She took a moment to study him. Contradictions. Maybe that was why she felt so confused right now. He was wild, but steady. Unpredictable, but so solid. Someone she could rely on. And yet, she would never be able to control him. Nor would she try.

Some women wanted a man they could train. One they could manipulate into their way of thinking, even if that wasn't their intention. Ellie wanted nothing to do with that. If pressed, she'd have said she wanted someone strong who would stand beside her.

But the reality was, that thought scared her more than a man who was...malleable. She had no idea what she would even do if she had a friendship that developed into more.

How could she go into something like that without making a mess of it the way she had done with every other relationship in her life so far?

It wasn't worth the pain of trying.

After the disastrous end to her college experience, Ellie had determined that she was going to lay low. Work was enough of a distraction. She regularly took the Christmas and Thanksgiving shifts so the other deputy and the sheriff could be with their families. She hung out with her dad after the holidays, or he would come by the office and bring her a slice of pie from the diner.

Her dad.

Ellie slid out her phone. She pulled up his number from her recent calls and waited for it to ring. He never picked up lately. She was getting tired of him ducking her calls. Of him forcing her to figure this out herself when she really needed his help.

When it went to voicemail, she said, "Dad, it's me. When you get this message call me *immediately*."

Drew said, "You think the sheriff can help?"

Former sheriff, but a lot of people still referred to him that way. Interesting that Drew did also. Usually it meant they'd met him in his official capacity—as the sheriff of this county from before she was born, all the way to after she left for college.

"I guess not?"

"What?" She focused on him and realized she'd been seriously drifting.

"Your dad."

"Oh. I was thinking about something else."

"Related to all this?" He pointed at the cabin.

"No. Just a…hard time I had." Mistakes. Things she never should have done. And then, the devastating conse-quences.

To say she'd been scarred by it was probably an understatement. Clear indication that she definitely shouldn't be looking at Drew and thinking about relationships at the same time. There was *no way* that would ever end up a good thing for her.

He started to say something else, but his phone rang. "I need to take this."

She waved him off. It wasn't like he needed to babysit her and her fractured state of mind. She'd been shot at, had run for her life, fought for her life, and been cut with a knife. It was like everything that could have gone wrong in one day had gone wrong.

She let out a heavy sigh and kept walking. To the field, where crops had grown years ago. A ramshackle barn. Empty now and littered with leaves that had blown in the open door. Void of life. Like the decision she'd made to steer clear of relationships other than what she had with her father and Laney.

Was this what she had decided?

———

"From what I found," Mark said on the other end of the line, "Brad and Sheila Traveston are in Acapulco."

"What?"

"Yeah, I did some digging. Pulled our tech support in on it. They left two weeks ago, return flights booked for another week from now. Also, incidentally, the techs found an account in one of the biggest banks in Mexico."

"Money?" Drew saw Ellie glance over at him, but couldn't explain when he himself didn't even know the extent of what Mark had found yet. "And a vacation?"

"A hundred thousand dollars. The account is in their

names, and they accessed it yesterday. Pulled out ten thousand in cash."

"Way to vacation."

Mark chuckled. "Right?"

The last vacation Drew had been on, Mark had convinced him that they should go deep-sea fishing off the coast of Washington. Four days of freezing cold, pouring rain, and fish.

Fishing with a pole on the side of the lake in *summer* was one of his favorite things. That vacation with Mark? Not so much. Fishing as a teen was where Uncle Merrick had told him all about his life. And planted the bug of living on his own terms, making money by bringing in criminals determined to escape justice.

Drew said, "So they were paid for the house."

"Some kind of payment was made to them. I'm not sure if it was the value of their property, or their silence. Maybe they were forced to take it and leave, and it's all they've got now."

He said, "Did you find any of the others?"

"Yeah." Mark was quiet for a few seconds, then said, "Here they are. Two others with Mexican bank accounts. One in Belize. All people who moved away from that dinky town of yours in the last few years."

"Only I'm allowed to call it that."

"Any-way," Mark dragged out the word. "I'm sure it's lovely. But people are running from it. At least, that's what it looks like from my end. Checks handed out from that company, far larger than the value of the property in some cases. Then there are the gifts. Dividend payouts. Kids' college savings accounts. Grants. Scholarships."

"Smells like bribe money to me."

"Exactly," Mark said. "Any way you can think of

someone coming into money and not having to pay income tax on it, these people got it. Except one."

"My father?"

"No—" Mark cut himself off. "Your *father?*"

"There's more to this than what I put in that email. But we can talk about that later."

"Okay." He didn't sound satisfied, though. Mark was the kind of guy who got an itch and didn't quit scratching until it hurt. Painful—not to mention gross—but effective. Mark said, "One more. A death certificate for a 55-year-old woman who died in a car accident. She used to live in town. It was ruled as having no particular cause. She just veered off the road and hit a tree, head on."

"And you believe it's legit?" Drew figured it was more likely that someone else caused her to swerve and lose control. If she hadn't been under the influence of something that might've impaired her judgment, that is.

"I've seen more suspicious death certs than this one."

Drew pressed his lips together. "Doesn't mean it's nothing."

"And your father?"

He pressed his lips together. "What I need from you right now is information about who is in on this with Simon Mills. It can't just be him if it's been going on for years, people forcing other people out of their homes." He looked at what remained of the home he'd lived in for nearly fifteen years. "And for what?"

Cashing in on a house that wasn't here? This had to be more than fraud.

Now was hardly the time to run a theory he had by Mark. And that was all it was. Maybe not even a theory. It could be nothing more than wishful thinking that his father might have…what? Killed himself for a *good* reason?

"When you were given clearance to be a contractor, we

looked into you." He was quiet for a second, then said, "I know your father killed himself."

"That isn't what this is about," Drew said.

He could detach his emotions long enough to realize he wanted closure over his father's death. This was all hitting way too close to home. Finding that eviction notice and then being at Lookout Point right when bullets started flying.

People forced out of their homes.

A woman in an "accident," and people being paid off.

There was definitely something he was missing, and whether or not it all tied back to his father committing suicide was a good question. Or maybe he'd even been murdered. Well, what would that mean? Would it change anything about Drew's life now, knowing that?

He could find the person responsible. But even if there was justice, it wouldn't change anything. He'd lived for years with the fact his only remaining parent was gone. And he would carry that until the day he died. God had blessed him with new "parents." Drew had found a way to love them. To accept the love they wanted to give him.

If God wanted to add more to his life, he would find a way to make that relationship a part of his life as well.

The past couldn't change. All Drew could do now was make every day count. To choose the things that made today better, decisions that would have positive repercussions for the rest of his life.

"I'll keep looking into Northcorp Inland Holdings."

"Thanks," Drew said. "I appreciate—"

"DREW!"

He spun around, but couldn't see Ellie. Was she okay?

Mark said something, but Drew didn't hear what it was. He said, "Gotta go," hung up, then raced around the half-collapsed cabin calling out, "Ellie!"

At the front corner he nearly ran into her. She didn't look

hurt, but her eyes were wide. "What is it?" He reached out. She grasped both his arms and clung to him. "Ellie. Did you see someone?"

"Yeah, you could say that." She blew out a breath and shook her head. Like she'd worked through the surprise and gotten herself together. He didn't blame her for being thrown, but this was the cop he knew she was, underneath the fear. A woman capable of bringing down a knife-wielding man intent on doing her harm. Who took the hits, processed the fear, and got back to work.

She took another breath and stepped back from him. "Stay where I can see you."

"What's going on?" He looked around but couldn't see anything that would've made her yell for him like she had.

"I found something. So don't wander off for a minute."

Her voice had a tone, one he didn't like at all. What was she insinuating? He frowned. She walked to her vehicle and stood with the door open while she grabbed her radio and called in. "Dispatch, come back."

He moved close enough he could hear both ends of the conversation. All the while she kept her gaze on him and the cabin. He turned to the front door. What was she looking at?

"What's your situation, Deputy Maxwell?"

Ellie gave the address, then said, "I've got a dead body out here."

Drew spun around. There was a body?

The voice on the other end of the radio said, "Uh…" There was a pause, then the voice on the other end of her radio said, "Copy that." Unsure now. Not a situation that happened for the department in this county very often. Maybe that was why she'd reacted the way she did to the surprise of discovering a dead body.

"Inside the cabin, hidden from view. Mostly," Ellie called out. "I didn't see it until I walked back to the front, going the opposite way around." She shook her head, liked she'd seen a huge spider out the corner of her eye and freaked out. But she'd pulled it together fast.

He had to walk almost all the way to the front door. Two broken porch steps. Then he saw it.

He saw *her*.

A dead woman, lying on the floor of his home.

7

Ellie took two steps toward the cabin. Cold moved through her. She might have been a sheriff's deputy for years, but she hadn't seen many dead bodies. And the first thing she'd done? Call for Drew.

She'd been walking around the cabin. On edge because she'd thought she had seen something moving in the woods —a predator on two legs, or four. She wasn't sure. She hadn't wanted to get shot at again, so she'd been tense.

Then she'd glanced in the door and saw the pale skin. The outstretched hand. She'd reacted—and not in a way she was proud of.

She pushed out a breath and tried to brush off the indignity of reacting like that. Her. A sheriff's deputy.

Drew matched her steps. She stopped and turned to him. "You need to stay back."

"Okay." His face was blank.

Whatever he was thinking, she couldn't tell what it was. Did she want to know? Right now she had to set aside her own feelings and properly process this body. Give the dead woman the respect she deserved—the kind of respect every person deserved. Dignity was a human right.

What she didn't have time for was Drew's emotion. He was a grown man and from the sound of what he'd told her so far, he was well versed in police procedure. He should know there was now a whole list of things she needed to do.

Ellie checked her watch. Maybe one of these days she'd get overtime pay for a good reason and not a terrible one. But that wasn't likely to happen in this line of work.

Thoroughly distracted by the random train of thoughts, Ellie took one more breath. When she pushed it out, the air puffed white in front of her. She moved toward the front door, pulling on a pair of protective gloves, and stepped between the frame and the door, which was leaning half-in and half-out of the structure. Or what was left of it.

Animals and leaves had both blown in during bad weather. Hopefully the animals at least were gone right now. Ellie's nose wrinkled before she even registered the smell, though it was so cold there wasn't much odor to speak of. More of a tang. She moved closer and assessed the area around the body.

And then she saw the face.

"Drew." She called out this time, not in the frightened way she had before.

"What is it?" His voice was closer, but he wasn't in the cabin. This had been his childhood home. Was he dealing with memories, as well as the details of this case? Maybe she should try and have some compassion for him. Instead, she was getting frustrated over her own failures; taking it out on him.

She moved back to the doorway and saw him standing in the dirt at the bottom of the porch steps. Leaning down, looking under the porch roof that had collapsed on one side.

Her stomach churned. Death was not something she

could pass off like no big deal the way some cops were able to. She'd never have made it as a homicide detective, and she knew that. Ellie understood and had come to terms with her shortcomings.

She said, "It's the receptionist. From the real estate agency office. Natalie Benson."

His eyebrows lifted. "Seriously?"

"I think she was shot." Ellie glanced back at the body. Once in the chest, at least.

She heard him start to say something, but the sound of an engine cut him off. "It's the sheriff."

Ellie nodded. This death couldn't be a coincidence. They'd spoken with this woman earlier today. A lot had happened since then, but there was no way their questions hadn't drawn attention in a town this small.

The receptionist had given them nothing, though. Did Natalie Benson ask questions of someone else, and they'd shot her because of it? Ellie had only asked her where Simon Mills was so that she could talk to him. As far as they'd known, purely because of lack of evidence, the receptionist was not part of any of this.

Simon Mills was the one listed on the company board. What part had this woman played? In whatever capacity she was involved, the cost had been grave.

Ellie ducked under the frame of the door. She met the sheriff halfway from his truck and explained everything. There was no point in beating around the bush right now. Not when he needed context.

By the time she was done explaining, with Drew adding details here and there, the sheriff's jaw was clenched.

"You think all of that adds up to something?"

"You don't?" She lifted her hands then let them fall to her sides.

"What I think is that we have a dead woman here, and

the medical examiner is on his way. So we best get to processing the scene."

What he meant, was that *she* should get to processing the scene. So that was what she did, grabbing the bag from the back of her vehicle and lugging it to the cabin. Photos, evidence collection. Notes. This was going to take hours.

She shot Drew a glance. He seemed more worried about her than the fact he stood there with nothing to do. Shame she couldn't have him help, but he wasn't authorized.

Maybe she should talk to the sheriff about having him deputized. Would he accept?

The idea that they could work together officially was an interesting thought. One she'd have quite liked to mull over with a cup of decaf coffee on her couch, covered in the throw blanket her mother had knitted while she was going through chemo.

Ellie unzipped the bag and started pulling out what she needed. She should call her dad again but not to leave another voicemail. It had been long enough since she left the last one that she was getting worried. She'd told him it was urgent. The former sheriff of this county should've at least been aware that a questionable company was forcing locals from their homes and buying up their land. He had to know something.

And for what? Certainly not so they could build condos, or the like. Though maybe that had happened elsewhere. Perhaps there was something else that made this land here valuable. A mine, or possibly fracking. Something they couldn't see from the house. She had a few ideas what it could be, but that was also *all* she had. Ideas. Taking a hike through the land might yield an answer.

There was something going on, though. *That* she could be sure of. Otherwise they wouldn't have triggered the shooting the first night, Drew's tires being slashed or those two guys in the truck, paid to make life miserable for them. Alone, those incidents could be explained away. All together they added up to something.

And now that they had a dead body on their hands, it was adding up to a whole lot more than just "something."

She moved back to the door and called out, "Drew."

He looked up from his phone.

"Don't feel like you have to stick around. I'm going to be hours."

The sheriff strode toward him. "Actually, I'd like a word." Her boss didn't acknowledge her. The two men moved far from her. Out of earshot.

Ellie couldn't even read their lips, though they were having an intense conversation by the look of it. What was going on? There was no time to ask if she had any hope of getting home before dark tonight. Being out in the open had freaked her out once already today.

Home was safe.

Until now, she'd have said this whole town was home. Now that she'd been attacked, more than once, the place she'd always felt safe suddenly didn't seem so comforting.

Where are you, Dad?

She needed to find him. Make sure he was all right.

Fight the fear, and figure this out.

———

"She approached me about this."

The sheriff shot him a look. "And you wouldn't have gone digging into it on your own?"

Drew kind of wished he had. That way, Ellie wouldn't have a knife wound on her arm. She hid the pain well, but it had to be bothering her. Kind of like the fact they'd been…

she had been ambushed. Her life in danger. Shot at, attacked with a knife.

His tires had been slit. That was more of an annoyance than anything else. With Ellie, they weren't messing around. The incidents where her life was threatened could have caused her to be seriously hurt, if not killed.

Slit tires were a warning.

Murder was something else entirely.

Drew didn't like any of it. Enough he was tempted to call Mark on one of the many favors his FBI agent friend owed him. He had saved Mark's life many times. Not to mention getting the man results on whatever case he was stuck on. Evidence. Surveillance. Drew had done it all, and he was better at it than he'd ever imagined.

But he still liked the freedom of working for himself. The FBI bureaucracy, and the structure of the organization, was way too much like the military for Drew to do well there. He knew that about himself, at least. And it was why he'd remained only a contractor with a solid contact list of associates. People he'd worked with. People he trusted. People who also owed him favors.

Seeing that knife flash in Ellie's direction made him want to bring them all in. Didn't matter how much it cost him.

Question was, who did he ask first?

"That's what I thought." The sheriff shot him a smug look.

Drew hardly even knew what the man was talking about, he'd been so deep in his own thoughts. "Ellie is in danger. Her life has been threatened twice in as many days."

"You think *Ellie* is going to accept protection?"

Drew didn't like the tone, the way he said her name. Or whatever he was trying to insinuate by saying it like that. "I think it's your job to keep your people safe."

"You wanna tell me what's my job?"

Drew took a breath, because it was better he do that now than get arrested in a minute. Though whatever he wound up being arrested for, it would likely feel immensely satisfying.

After he took a few breaths, staring at the cabin, he turned back to the sheriff. "If she gets hurt, it'll be on you."

Something flashed across the sheriff's face. Drew didn't know what it was. The older man said, "Maybe I should deputize you."

He knew what Drew did for a living—and who he did it with. Drew wasn't blind to the fact the sheriff had at some point taken the time to get all up in his business. He would have too if he'd been the one who was sheriff. But this man had never given such an offer before.

Drew shook his head. "You can't afford my rates."

That didn't mean he wasn't going to provide around the clock protection for her, completely free of charge. That was how much he owed her father for finding him after his dad died. First thing he'd done was gently break the news. Then he'd had him pack. After that, he'd driven him straight over to the house where he lived now. Eric and Alma's house.

He'd never been given a better gift in his life.

And yet, the sheriff—Ellie's father—had kept coming around. Not all the time, more like every few months. Sometimes longer than that. *Just checkin' in.* Like he cared about Drew and wanted to know how he was doing.

The current sheriff had been a few years ahead of Drew in school. Football team captain. Trophies. All-State champions. That kind of stuff. If there had been a pool at their school, Drew would have tried out for the swim team. But there hadn't been.

"You talked to the receptionist this morning," the sheriff said, like that would be news to Drew. "That's where you were when your tires were slashed."

He nodded. "Ellie is the one who talked to her. Though, why asking about Simon Mills would have led to her getting shot at is anyone's guess."

He had no idea. So far everything that had happened could be explained away as someone's attempt to warn them. Shoot at her but not kill her. Slash Drew's tires. Those two guys with their knife were a little more serious escalation of things. A way to get them to back off the questions they were asking?

The sheriff said, "You think Natalie Benson mentioned it to the wrong person?"

"Yeah, I do."

Who that was, Drew had no idea.

"Like you said, if she gets hurt that'll be on *you*."

"Ellie?" Drew waited. When the sheriff nodded, he said, "I'm going to make sure she's safe while she does her job and investigates this murder." He folded his arms. "What are you going to do?"

"My job."

Drew didn't want to ask what exactly that was. He didn't think that would get him a helpful answer. It occurred to him that if Ellie's father knew who was behind all the land being purchased, it stood to reason this man did as well. But how did you go about accusing a sheriff of being on the take? And the previous sheriff, Ellie's father and a man he'd respected? Drew would need conclusive evidence if he was going to make an accusation like that.

Threats of repercussions, if the accusations were true, weren't going to be much better than accusing him outright, so Drew didn't do that either.

"You find Simon Mills," Drew said, "and get word to me first."

"Now why would I go and do that?"

"Because you don't want to be associated with this." He

waved at the cabin, meaning the dead body. But also Ellie and all that was happening with her. "We wouldn't want the wrong people getting word that you are digging up something that should stay under the surface."

The sheriff worked his jaw back and forth. "Okay. You get that, but it's a short leash."

"Ellie isn't going to let me go off half-cocked and put her job, or anyone else, in jeopardy." And why was he suddenly acting like Drew would be a help in this situation? Had he finally come around?

"Murder changed it." The man's dark look said more than his words. This was life and death now.

Drew nodded. The receptionist's death meant there was less margin for error now. This was serious. "Someone is willing to kill to protect their secret. You don't want to put *your* job in jeopardy, and I get that." Drew had more leeway and with a whole lot more autonomy given, there were less regulations. Just the law. Comparatively, the sheriff's hands were tied.

Drew said, "But I want anything and everything you can give me on these people. And what they're up to."

"Sometimes cancer is so deeply imbedded, the only way to get it out is to destroy everything."

Drew had no idea if that analogy actually made medical sense, but he got the idea. "I do this, there's no fallback on you." He paused. "Question is, do you want it done?"

"I want my deputy safe."

"And whoever's buying the land, forcing people out of their homes?"

The skin around the sheriff's eyes contracted. As though he hated even hearing the words spoken aloud. "How do you know they didn't *want* to leave?"

"Ellie mentioned Sheila and Brad. There have to be others, but we haven't found anyone to even talk to. Coincidence?" He let that hang. "And they weren't just given payment for their property, they were given bribe money. Who knows if that amount was even fair market value?"

"Find the cancer, and get it out of my town." He walked away, leaving Drew standing by himself. He then moved to the cabin and went inside.

A minute later Ellie walked out, pulling off her gloves. "What was that about? It looked pretty heated."

"He's worried, that's all. Doesn't like murder."

"Does anyone?"

Drew seized the opportunity and cracked a smile. "Maybe a psycho. But that's probably it."

"Short list." She returned his smile. "So what now? He told me to clock out and get some rest. Which is really weird…"

Before she could go on, prolonging the conversation about her boss's behavior, he said, "How about dinner first?"

She blinked at him.

He shrugged. "I'm hungry."

"I have some of my dad's pot roast in the freezer," she said. "It's probably still good." She was inviting him over? "We can lay out what we have and see if we missed anything."

Ah. Keeping things professional. Drew said, "Sounds good. We do need a plan."

They walked to their vehicles. Ellie glanced over before she rounded the hood of her car. "I'd be able to think better if I didn't have this itchy feeling on the back of my neck." Drew glanced around but didn't see anyone watching them.

"Exactly." She frowned. "Feels like someone is spying on us."

Like whoever had killed that young woman lying dead in the cabin. Drew wanted to get out of there and somewhere safe as soon as possible. "Let's go."

8

"It's in here somewhere." Ellie shoved aside a Ziploc bag of pizza slices she should have tossed out a few days ago and found it. "Ah-ha."

She turned to find Drew across the other side of her kitchen. Yes, he was close enough in the tiny space she could reach out and touch him. If he reached out as well.

He shook his head. "What?"

"Nothing." She turned her back to him, because the microwave was above the stove. Not for any other reason… like the fact that he was here and making her antsy. Aside from her father, she'd never had a man in her kitchen. And she'd lived here for years.

Ellie didn't know if that was noble, or incredibly sad. She probably wouldn't like the answer.

She typed on the microwave keypad, jabbing buttons so hard she was going to break them one of these days. "My dad is an awesome cook. You're gonna love this."

"I know he is."

She spun around. "What do you mean, you know?"

Drew looked entirely too smug for her liking. Or, maybe

it wasn't that he looked smug. Maybe just pleased with himself. Because she was uncomfortable? What kind of guy got satisfaction from throwing a woman off kilter?

She folded her arms. She was starting to think dinner had been a bad idea. "Explain."

He shot her a look, lips curled up. Like he thought she was cute. "A few years back I spent Thanksgiving with your dad. You were off at college, I think. Somewhere. I didn't have plans and I was between contracts. When he found out, he swung by my house and invited me." Drew paused. "So, yes. I know he's a good cook."

"Oh." The microwave beeped. Ellie swung the door open and grabbed the dish.

It was hot.

She hissed, clutching the ceramic bowl. For a second, her brain stuttered. She didn't know what to do with the dish and the fact it was burning her hands.

"Here." Drew pulled the towel from the rail and grabbed the dish with the protection of the dish towel between his skin and the stoneware.

Ellie took a breath. "Ouch."

"Run your hands under the faucet. But only lukewarm. Not cold."

Oh-kay. Was he Mr. Come to the Rescue or what? Ellie did as he'd instructed, watching him out the corner of her eye. When he opened the wrong cupboard, she said, "This side," and tipped her head back.

He scooted between her and the refrigerator on the far wall, moving to the cupboard she'd indicated. He took down two bowls with those strong hands of his, his forearms flexing.

She blinked. Forearms?

It was official. She was losing it.

This dinner seriously needed to get back to business territory, and fast. Otherwise she was going to have a nervous breakdown over the notion that she might be attracted to Drew.

Okay, so she was. But was that the point? Hardly. There was nothing that was going to happen between them. Her head knew that. It was logical. Correct. She needed to fall back on the conclusions she'd arrived at.

Relationships, bad.

Solitude, good.

Work, good.

Tell that to her feelings, though. They didn't seem to want to listen to reason at all, no matter how much she tried to remind herself that Drew was a man. She wasn't threatened. But her heart couldn't take another beating. Not after what had happened when she'd been *away at college.*

Evidently Drew had been eating Thanksgiving dinner with her father.

The one Thanksgiving break she hadn't come home was because she was too busy dealing with her life and how it had suddenly turned upside down.

What happened next had destroyed any plans she'd made for Christmas. Her dad had ended up spending that one with her.

In the hospital.

"You okay?"

She glanced over, frowning at the gentle voice he used. The soft look on his face wasn't helpful either.

"Are you worried because he hasn't called you back yet?"

Ellie nodded. Yes, she was worried and needed to hear from him, before she lost control of everything else. She moved to her phone and looked at the screen. Not that she'd have missed a call.

They sat at her tiny table with its two chairs. If she

wanted to eat with both Laney *and* her father, then they went to his house.

Ellie took the first bite as she realized for the first time how narrow her life was. Not that it was an especially bad thing. She actually quite liked the controlled way she lived. Work, her family—which included her best friend. Now Drew, and this case.

When it was over, he would retreat back to his corner of town. And his contracts with the feds. They would go back to not seeing each other.

Ellie would go back to her life.

"You were right. It is good."

She tried to smile at Drew, but she couldn't quite make her heart do that right now.

"Tell me." There was something in his eyes.

She wanted to just say it. Everything. Tell him all of it.

His phone rang.

The look on his face was noteworthy. Enough that she almost smiled then. He swiped it up, glaring daggers at the device. "What?"

The voice on the other side had a low tone, but she couldn't make out the words.

"Fine. You can tell Ellie too. I'll put it on speaker."

He jabbed at the button. The voice kept talking. It came through with, "…seriously." Then he paused. "Hello?"

"Mark, this is Ellie." Drew scooped up a chunk of potato with his fork. "Ellie, meet FBI Assistant Director Welvern." He stuck the potato in his mouth.

"Hi, Mark."

"Hello, Ellie." It almost sounded like he was trying not to laugh.

"You have something?" She could have left the silence, but she preferred to put people out of their misery. Mostly because she would want someone to do that for her.

"Uh—" He cleared his throat. "—yes. I ran the dead receptionist's full name and her driver's license number. Local girl, as of a year ago. Moved, after she got fired from her office job in the city. The job she has now, at the real estate office, was advertised through a recruitment website."

"The job she *had*."

Drew shot her a dark look.

Ellie tipped her head to the side.

He shook his. "So it wasn't advertised locally, but cast with a wider net instead?" In this small town everyone posted jobs in the classified section of the newspaper. Or on that bulletin board at the grocery store.

"Seems like it," Mark said.

"That doesn't mean it wasn't in the paper here in town. Easy enough to find out." Ellie let go of her spoon and sat back in her chair. She'd looked so cute and flustered earlier. Enough he'd gone against his better judgment and actually mentioned it. That could've been a catastrophe.

She said, "That's where most jobs around here are advertised."

Drew read the paper every morning. "But if Simon Mills was looking all over, could be he wanted someone from out of town. Someone who wouldn't know that things in town weren't as they should be."

Ellie lifted her chin. "Someone who wouldn't care when locals were turned out on their ear because someone wanted to buy their land."

And they still didn't know *why* Northcorp Inland Holdings was purchasing property around town. Drew said, "Did you get the information on what exactly they own?"

"It's all concentrated to the north and west."

Ellie said, "Maybe a highway, or new bypass? They're trying to cash in on the government needing to buy up land for a new road? Or some kind of vacation resort."

"That's a serious long game." One that had been years in the making so far. And how long would it take for the government to decide where to put a road? "Once word is passed down about the plan in place, then the right person hears it. They buy up what's going to be purchased first and then cash in big time. Isn't that how it goes?"

Ellie shrugged.

Mark said, "I'll send you what I have so you can check a map. Just looks like trees from what I'm seeing."

Only he and Ellie were close enough to the land to understand what possible significance it might have. From his office in Denver, Mark had a limited understanding.

"Thanks for your help."

"Guess you can scratch two off now."

Ellie frowned.

Drew said, "From the list of a million favors he owes me."

"Probably more like a hundred." Mark's voice, even through the phone, had a *tone*. One that made Drew laugh.

"Hundreds is more like it." Drew spoke around the smile he gave Ellie, and she returned it.

Mark hung up.

Drew wanted to ask her what she did to bleed off bad days on the job. Days like this, when she'd been put through the wringer. Maybe she didn't have many, so she didn't know how to deal with it.

Her father cooked to de-stress, and he was really really good at it. Which probably meant he'd had many bad days—enough to build those skills. What about Ellie? The initial curiosity was only deepening. He wanted to know everything about her.

Sitting at her tiny kitchen table in her little house one

time wasn't going to be enough. He wanted more. He was drawn to her, and not just to fulfill the promise he'd made to the sheriff that he was going to keep her safe.

It was more.

To the point that it was seriously testing his resolve to stay separate from the people in this town. After the life he'd had growing up, he never thought he'd actually come back and discover something more here.

Maybe that made him judgmental, but it seemed Ellie was going to be the one who changed his mind.

Eric and Alma didn't live here anymore. That only left two others in town. Her father hadn't managed it, despite the impact the old sheriff had had on his life. Ellie's best friend hadn't, either. Though, that was only a business relationship.

And despite them all, Drew still held himself back. Neither of them got through to the real him that he kept hidden. Being around Ellie made him relax. And maybe that was the key. He wanted to tell her everything about himself.

"Drew?"

"Yeah?" He shook off the depth of thoughts. "What is it?"

The frown was as cute as the rest of her, but he didn't think she'd agree. Something was bothering her. She said, "Was she killed because we showed up asking questions?"

"Did you ask her about the land being bought out?"

Ellie shook her head. "Just about the corporation. I also asked her where Simon was and when he would be back."

"And their response to our questions is murder?" He shook his head. "I don't buy that. It's not a good reason to silence someone. It won't stop us. Arguably it both draws attention to the fact that there really is something going on in town *and* they have to know we'll be more motivated now, since a woman is dead."

She nodded. Was she convinced though? Drew couldn't

tell. He stood and carried both their empty bowls to the sink. "Got any ice cream?"

She spun in her chair.

"It's my weakness."

That got him a smile. Still, she said, "I think we should go look around the real estate office. Before the sheriff sends someone over there."

He leaned his hips against the Formica countertop. "You think he'll do that tonight, or tomorrow morning?"

"Probably tomorrow, given the time. He'll want to talk to Simon as well."

"He's not the only one," Drew said. "I'd sure like to find him and ask him about all this."

"I can't believe the BOLO has come up with nothing so far."

"He's laying low." Drew thought for a moment, then said, "I'd have thought he would be looking for an alibi. Or he's already fled to Mexico." He sighed. "If we're going to be breaking and entering, you should get changed."

"I'm a sheriff's deputy, I'm not going to break and enter anything."

He held up his hands. "Sorry. My bad."

She blew out a breath. "I'd like to know where Simon Mills lives."

"Me too. From what Mark told me it's like the man literally does not exist."

"And today he happens to be absent from work?" Ellie got up and stretched. "Let's go see if we can find anything in his office that might indicate who he really is. Or where we can find him."

He stared at her.

"I'll call the sheriff. Make it an official visit."

That meant there would be restrictions on whether or not Drew would be able to pick the lock. Still, he nodded.

Honor was something in short supply in the work he usually did. Criminals didn't care if he was a nice guy. Drew's job was to get in, get what the feds needed, and get out.

Protecting Ellie—both keeping her safe and not putting her job in jeopardy—was going to be a different kind of task.

But one he was well equipped for, given his history. His career choices. The jobs he'd worked, and the kind of people he'd come up against. Whatever he and Ellie faced, Drew figured God would pick up the slack for whatever it was they couldn't handle.

He wasn't one of those guys who thought a woman couldn't protect herself. But he knew that together they would make sure she remained unscathed. *Help me do this, Lord.* His protective streak ran a mile wide. For a second, keeping her safe felt like it might be the most important job he'd ever have in his life.

Twenty minutes later they pulled up outside the real estate office. She hadn't changed. Still in uniform, Ellie cracked the door. She got out but stood between the door and the frame. Staring at the office.

"What is it?" He opened his own door. Then he smelled it. "Fire."

Not just a fire, but a man running away from the building.

Ellie yelled, "Hey! Stop!"

And then took off after him.

9

Ellie knew this town so well she could run through it blindfolded, though that wasn't generally recommended as it tended to cause accidents. The man ahead of her raced around the corner of the building. His shoes slipped, and he nearly went down. One arm shot out in order to catch his balance and then he disappeared into the alley between the Main Street storefronts.

She pumped her arms and legs, forced to ignore the sting of the knife wound on her arm. Didn't feel quite so superficial now that she needed to use that limb.

At the corner of the building she stopped. Pulled her gun, and took a split second to brace. Then she whipped around it, weapon first.

There was no sense in meeting an ambush without taking a second to be ready. Especially if this was the person who'd shot Natalie Benson and left her body in Drew's childhood home.

This wasn't the first time since they found her body that Ellie wondered if there was significance to leaving her there. It could be they'd purposely taken her somewhere they knew

Ellie and Drew would go. But that was a long shot. More likely it was out of the way enough they figured Natalie wouldn't be found for a long while.

They wanted her to be found.

Or they didn't.

Ellie wasn't sure which it was. Or whether it was significant that it had been Drew's place. Depended on ballistics and any other evidence the sheriff had collected.

The sight of a car pulled her back to focus on the chase. Ellie ran toward it, following the guy through the beam of headlights.

He was shorter than her. Small frame for a man. Could be a woman, but she didn't think so. More likely, she figured, he was a teenage boy.

Whoever he was, his hip glanced off the front corner of the car. The headlight went dark as he moved in front of it and headed for the passenger door.

"Stop!"

He was attempting to flee the scene of what she assumed was arson. Was this Simon? She didn't know how tall he was, but figured Simon wouldn't look like a teen boy from the back.

Or maybe Simon was back at the real estate office. Was he dead in there, his body about to be become ash?

Ellie planted her feet and yelled, "Sheriff's department! Stop!"

He needed to come to her. Most people surrendered when faced with an armed officer of the law. It was the rest of the population that were the problem. Not quite as inclined to cooperate. Where was Drew? She couldn't hear anyone behind her. Had he gone to the office? Was he calling in the fire? That would be helpful.

Not to mention how it felt to know he was aware she could take care of herself. He trusted her. Believed in her.

But that belief wasn't going to get this guy to come in quietly. Or any other way. Overconfidence never ended well.

She said, "Walk back to me. Slowly. Hands where I can see them."

He hesitated, one hand now on the door handle. Not armed. She figured he'd have shot her already if he had a gun.

He pulled open the door to the passenger…

He wasn't driving.

Where was the—

A dark figured rushed her. The bigger frame barreled into her so fast and hard Ellie's feet lifted off the ground. It felt like being hit by a semi-truck. Her arm swung up. She squeezed the trigger as she sailed through the air. The gun went off.

Ellie landed on her back on the concrete pavement. Her body exploded with pain. The gun skittered across the ground.

A suffocating weight settled on her chest. She tried to fight against it, struggling to breath. She pushed, but her arms were pinned to her sides. She tried to kick, but he was massive. And right on top of her.

Anger burned in her stomach. She couldn't handle weakness any better than she could handle things being out of her control. Both birthed hot frustration in her. It came out as a thick roar from her throat.

Hands banded around her neck. She blinked against an explosion of bright lights across the black of night.

The sound from her mouth cut off. Air got stuck in her throat. The squeeze of his hands on her neck was all she could think about. Her world coalesced to nothing but the feel of his thick fingers tight around her throat.

Drew.

She needed him right now. She kicked but didn't have the

strength to get the guy off her. She couldn't even roll. He probably weighed close to two hundred fifty pounds. She had muscle—and more weight than she needed on her five-seven frame—but it wasn't helping.

She wanted to scream but had no air in her lungs.

His hot breath brushed her face, and she heard a chuckle from somewhere far away. "…good for me. Means I don't have to find you and kill you later."

"Ellie!" Drew's voice rang out as he approached.

Did he see her? She tried to call out to him the way she had at the cabin but no sound came out of her mouth.

The man pinning her down stilled.

The car engine revved.

"Stop!" Drew's voice was clear even over the sound of horsepower surging. "Hey—"

A sickening thud. Everything in her went cold. Drew. *Lord…*

She didn't know what to say. Couldn't think of the words to convey the situation to a God she'd abandoned at the lowest point of her life. Would He even want to hear from her?

Maybe he would, considering it was about Drew. Didn't selflessness make it more valid? Like it wasn't for her own personal gain, so God should listen.

Help him.

Unconsciousness rushed up on her. Ellie didn't know how much longer she could hold out against the squeeze of his hands on her throat. *Help…me.*

Deep in her pocket, Ellie's phone started to vibrate.

She wanted to scream out all the frustration boiling hot in her stomach. A single tear ran from the corner of her eye into her hair. She could hardly see. Strength surged from somewhere, she didn't know where, and she kicked. Fought against him. Probably some last survival instinct coming to her aid.

The last of her strength.

"Ask too many questions, and you get dead." Spit landed on her face.

Ellie kept up her furious struggle.

Then her arm was free, and she had to shove away the surprise. She had no time to acknowledge and jabbed her fingers out straight. Right at his face.

He cried out.

Now both her arms were free. His grip on her neck was still deadly. She couldn't get his fingers off her. And she would end up dying while she tried to pry them free. Instead, she felt around her. Reaching for her gun, though she had no idea how far away it had fallen.

Her fingers grasped something hard. Sharp. Whatever it was, she grabbed it in a tight hold and swung it at his face.

The man cried out and fell off her.

Finally he let go of her neck, and she sucked in a full breath. As much air as she could through her constricted windpipe. *Thank You.* She tried to scramble up.

He crawled away, clutching his face. This homicidal maniac. Who was he?

"You're under arrest!" The words came out no louder than a whisper.

He rolled over and hefted himself up to his feet.

And then he ran away.

Ellie tried to stand. She fell back to the ground in a thud. "Drew."

———

"Ellie."

The car had hit him. Drew tried to get his leg underneath him. The limb buckled, but he pressed a hand against the side of the brick building and braced his weight. He winced at the poke of brick and concrete. Hopped.

Tried to walk.

He cried out, forced to fight against the urge to fall back to the ground. "Ellie!" Focusing on her was the only thing that kept him from going down.

He couldn't have broken his leg or anything else that serious. Otherwise he wouldn't be able to even limp. Extreme stubbornness didn't make a broken bone weight-bearing all of a sudden. Which meant it wasn't that bad.

Not that bad.

He repeated it. Life-giving words that were going to get him to where he was going.

Sirens in the distance revived him. Forced more energy and determination into his screaming body. His hip. His knee. Maybe his whole left side would be purple tomorrow. *Just promise me no internal bleeding.* The last thing he needed was to be incapacitated, or in surgery, when he was supposed to be protecting Ellie.

And now it was clear she needed watching.

Except that it was precisely what he was supposed to have been doing and look how spectacularly he'd failed? So much pride. Thinking he had the skills to keep her safe just because of missions. The first chance he'd had to do what he said he would—and could—he'd totally messed it up by checking for victims in the real estate office first.

Both of them had nearly died.

"Drew!"

She was there in front of him, her hands grasping his arms. They nearly collapsed together to the ground. "Ellie."

He forced his right knee to lock and hold most of his weight on that side.

"He tried to strangle me." She sucked in a breath that didn't sound good. "The car."

He tugged her toward the end of the alley. "Fire department should be here by now." He wanted to carry her. He *should* have picked her up and taken her to meet them. Instead, the truck pulled up outside the real estate office, and the fire fighters poured out in time to see Ellie helping him walk.

"Deputy?"

"We need an ambulance."

"Copy that." He trotted back to the truck and got on the radio.

"Over there." Drew spotted a bench, and they hobbled to it. Well, she wheezed and he hobbled. When he settled onto it, he couldn't bite back the cry.

"I think you're really hurt."

Drew didn't want to admit that, so he bit down on his molars. He tried to breathe through the pain enough he'd be able to see straight when the ambulance got there. No way were they going to push him on a gurney when he was conscious. He could walk. Mostly.

Turned out they didn't agree with him. Ellie left him to go get her gun, ensuring they treated him first. When she walked back over, he was in the ambulance. That was something, at least. "Come on." He waved her over so she could get in as well.

She shook her head and let out a little cough. "I'll meet you there."

"You need to get checked out."

"The fire department guys are trained. I can have one of them look at my neck. I want to know if they find anything in the office."

He didn't have time to object. The EMT shut the ambulance doors. Then it was a blur of lights. The prick of a needle. Drew let out a long breath. He should call the sheriff and tell him Ellie was at the real estate office, and he couldn't watch her.

Drew patted his pockets, but didn't find… His phone was in his truck. The one they'd driven here together. He had his wallet on him but nothing else. Not even his keys.

It was hours before they were done with x-rays and tests —most of which involved the doctor poking him in places he was sore while muttering to himself.

Drew said, "Don't even think about admitting me." When the doctor looked up, he added, "And have someone get me a phone. I need to call the sheriff."

The doctor left the room shaking his head. Two frustrating minutes later the nurse came in. "I hear you don't love our company."

"I need a phone."

He swung his legs off the side of the bed.

"If your feet even touch the floor, I'll tell the doctor you passed out and he'll admit you overnight."

Drew shot her a look. She wouldn't.

But he held his feet off the floor. It took too much strength and, after a few seconds, he had to sag back on the bed. He blew out a breath. "I really do need a phone."

"I'll be back with your discharge papers." Nurse Friendly flung the door open.

She left, but it didn't shut. A man entered. Someone who looked slightly familiar, but Drew couldn't place him. Not Simon Mills. Which was a shame.

"Not looking so good." The man had silver hair, and he was dressed in a suit. Shiny shoes. Not a man who got dirty on his way up the ladder—this guy was at the top.

"I bounce back quickly," Drew said. Who was he? "What do you want?"

"Cooperation. Understanding."

"We can't all have what we want." This guy was one of them. Drew knew it like he knew Ellie was probably the only woman in the world who might understand how he truly felt about the town. Drew continued, "Like a phone to call the sheriff."

"Not sure why you'd need to call the sheriff," the man said. "Unless you think I'm a threat." He bit off that last word. "And why would that be, when we can both benefit from an arrangement?"

From slashing his tires to getting recruited? They were feeling him out, and this guy was going to make an offer. But why? Was there dissension in the group, different people doing their own thing, or had someone changed their mind?

"The alternative is we kill both of you."

"We leave you alone, you leave us alone," Drew said. "Is that it?"

"It can be." The man stood straight at the end of the bed. He had the guts—or confidence—to come in here and make this pitch in what was a public place. Like these people thought they were untouchable. Paying people to hurt Ellie. To shoot at her.

Who was this guy? "What do you want?"

"Information. You tell me what she knows, and who she's told. In exchange, you are left alone."

"Not good enough," Drew said. "*In exchange*, no one else gets hurt. That's the only deal I'm going to agree to."

The man's mouth split into a smile more like a sneer.

Drew tried to get his brain to process all of this. Before the guy left, before it was too late. Ellie would get hurt if he didn't play this the right way. Drew hardly cared about his own life. Only a couple of people would miss him if he wasn't here anymore. Ellie had more than that. She made Malvern County a better place.

"Work with us, and this will go your way," the man said.

What was their endgame? Land…but for what?

"Keep her away from our business."

Ellie was a threat to them. As though she'd gotten too close without even realizing it, and now they wanted to know what she knew. They wanted her contained.

Drew wanted her safe. He bit down on his molars, knowing he would regret this when he had to tell her what he'd done. But also knowing he would do next to anything to keep her safe.

Without thinking over why that was so strong in him, he said, "Just as long as she's safe."

It was all that mattered.

10

"You did *what?*" Ellie couldn't believe what she was hearing. She could hardly talk around the swelling in her throat. They'd told her what signs to watch for and that she wasn't in the clear yet, but there was no way she was staying in the hospital.

Everything she'd been through and a little sore throat could kill her? She hadn't even known that swelling could come back later to do her in. Days later. There wasn't time for that.

"Will you sit down?" Drew waved at the end of the hospital bed.

Ellie did, but only because she was exhausted and her neck hurt. It was a mass of red marks and bruises already. Tomorrow it was going to look even worse—bad enough she might have to dig out that old turtleneck from the back of her closet.

She sighed. "He could have killed you."

Drew shook his head. "That wasn't why he was here."

"So he offered you a job instead?"

"In a way. It's a business arrangement, nothing more. They want to know what you know, presumably because you got so close to what they're doing that they got spooked."

Too bad she had no idea what exactly she'd stumbled on, or discovered. She had been trying to figure out what happened to Brad and Sheila. What—or rather, who—forced them off their land and made them feel they had to leave town and vacation in Mexico before starting their new life somewhere else?

She'd run some searches at work through the law enforcement databases they had access to. And she had called a friend at the state police to see if he had any reports or complaints logged. That could hardly have been sufficient to get them so worried. What had triggered all this?

"It's better than them coming after you to kill you."

"Again." She couldn't get the feel of that guy's fingers around her neck out of her mind. His dark words, the need to kill her. It sent a wave of cold through her that she might be their target, even while she had to acknowledge that the fact she was a threat to them meant she was doing her job.

That she was good at it.

It might be twisted to feel like that just because someone was trying to kill her, but she knew herself well enough to know it was true. It meant something to her. She wanted to be good at her job. She wanted to be looked up to, the way her dad had been. Ellie wanted people whose opinion mattered to be proud of her.

And maybe that included Drew.

Yet, he seemed determined to fix this himself.

"Look, I'll just put out feelers for now," he suggested. "There's no reason to jump in with both feet. They won't buy that anyway, not if they know the first thing about me."

She nodded. Anyone who knew he took federal contracts

might assume that undercover work was part of his gig. They could even surmise he was skilled enough to play both sides in order to get a result. Which meant he couldn't be fully trusted.

Ellie figured that at least she could trust him. Still, a tiny part of what was inside her—the part that had been destroyed through abandonment—worried that he might be playing her. Mostly she didn't believe it, but the worry did nag at her even though she didn't know why he would want to deceive her.

"Did you find anything in the real estate office?"

She shook her head. "No dead body. Just charred furniture."

"Paperwork? Could be they were trying to hide something."

She shrugged, wanting to sigh. Simon Mills was probably in Mexico as well. Paid off by whoever wanted her dead.

"You look exhausted." He swung his legs off the bed, dressed in his jeans and T-shirt. Feet covered with socks.

"Want me to find your shoes?"

"Please."

It wasn't like she wanted to talk about how she was doing. He could see that for himself, right? Worn out and beaten up. She needed about three days' worth of sleep and a mocha with about four extra shots.

She wound up tying his shoes for him, while a smile tugged at his lips. When she was done, she leaned back. "What?"

"Nothing." He shook his head and held out a hand.

Ellie took it, standing up the same time he did. Drew didn't manage to completely hide the wince when his knee was forced to take part of his weight.

He tugged her to him and slid his arms around her waist. His T-shirt was warm. Ellie pressed her cheek to it and hugged him back. Wow. This was nice. His hand rubbed up and down her back. She could get used to hugs if they felt like this.

The door opened. "Whoops…" The word dissipated, and the nurse said, "Are you *standing*?"

Drew pulled back from the hug. Ellie looked at the nurse holding a pair of crutches.

The nurse rolled her eyes. "You need these. To walk."

"Thanks," Drew said. When the nurse handed them over, he said to Ellie, "Wanna give me a ride home?"

"In your truck?"

"You're driving my truck?"

Uh-oh. That didn't look good. The nurse said, "I'm leaving your discharge papers. Y'all have fun working this out." The door shut, but not before she heard the woman chuckle.

Ellie said, "Was that not okay? I guess I could've walked over and borrowed a department vehicle. But it was right there."

Drew pulled her in again. "Don't worry about it."

He didn't care now? Ellie wasn't convinced he was okay with it but let it go since it seemed he was determined to do the same. *Oh-kay.*

She walked with him to the lobby and had him sit so she could bring his truck over. He didn't look happy when she suggested he sit but walked away before he had the chance to argue. She pulled up at the curb where he stood leaning on the crutches. When she came around and opened the passenger door, Drew handed the crutches to an orderly.

He got in the truck.

The orderly shot her a look. She shrugged and drove him to his house. "Do you need help with your horse tonight?"

He wasn't feeling well and probably didn't want to walk

around a bunch. She didn't want his horse to suffer because of it.

"Neighbor kid takes care of her when I'm out of town. I called him, so Spring is good."

Ellie nodded. She wasn't sure what else they should be talking about. Silence filled the cab of the truck. She tried to find something good on the radio, but no sound came out of the speakers.

"Doesn't work."

"Oh." She moved her hand back to the steering wheel. "I'll be at Laney's shop tomorrow. I help her with inventory every couple of weeks, and there's this North picture I've been eyeing. I think I'm going to get it." She shot him a smile. "I've had a bad enough week I can justify treating myself."

The photo was gorgeous. A sunset over the Rocky Mountains. He had to travel all over to be able to get the shots he took. Whoever he was, he was an amazing artist.

Ellie pulled up outside his house. When she turned to him, he had the weirdest look on his face. "You okay?"

"Yes." He grabbed the door handle and pulled on it. "I'll see you tomorrow, Ellie." At the last second, he shifted to turn back. "Be careful. Text me when you get home so I know you got there safe."

She wanted to ask him to do the same later, so she knew nothing happened. First time in her life she wanted to sit outside someone's house all night just to make sure they were okay. But doing that meant she'd be dragging all day tomorrow.

Ellie sat there for a while before she turned and drove his truck back to her house. On the way, she called her dad back. Phone tag was the most annoying thing. Made more annoying when he didn't pick up this time either.

What was he doing?

———

DREW HAD DECIDED before he even got out of his truck the night before. Now it was morning, and Ellie was in his drive again. At least what amounted to a drive in front of Eric and Alma's house. This time, at the wheel of her own little SUV.

He tugged the door open. "Thanks for picking me up."

"Sure you don't want to stay home today?" Her gaze shifted down to his knee, then back up.

"I'm sure." He climbed in, guiding his leg so he didn't twist his knee. He could mostly walk. "I need to be in town today."

Especially if she was going to be there. No point staying at home, licking his wounds and moaning about how much pain he was in. Better to distract himself with activity. Even if that meant nursing a cup of coffee while he watched over her work at Laney's shop.

Which had birthed his idea.

More of an intention, really. Drew wanted no more secrets between them. It was time she knew everything about him.

She sat silent while she drove. He could see the thoughts race through her mind. It was written on her face and in the way she bit her lip.

"Sleep okay?"

She shrugged one shoulder.

"About as good as me, then." He smiled, not sure why he felt so much lighter this morning. Because of his decision? She would finally have all the information she needed to make up her mind about him.

He could tell she was thinking about what to do. There was attraction between them. That hug had been sweet, and part of him wanted to know if there could be more than friendship here. Wanted to know if it was worth the risk to tell her everything.

She glanced over. "Still determined to put your life in jeopardy and get close to these people just to expose them?" Her voice had a *tone*. He didn't even know what to say to diffuse that.

Drew settled on, "Yes." Because it was the truth. "Those are the kinds of assignments Mark sends my way. Going in and getting him IDs, photos, and evidence. I don't look like a cop, and I don't act like a cop. I've also never been in the military."

She shot him a look.

"Cops and soldiers…" How did he explain it? "They have a *bearing* most people don't possess. Criminals can spot stuff like that. Their instincts for self-preservation are off the charts, as are their abilities to spot when someone is lying. Makes it hard for undercover work. So they send me in because I don't act like a fed."

She pulled into a space on Main Street and turned to him. "So you really are a contractor?"

"You thought I was lying about that?"

She shot him a look.

He said, "In essence, yes I am a contractor." He unbuckled his seatbelt. "Among other things. And that's why I know I can keep you safe as well as get what we need on these people." He paused. "We don't have the first clue who they are. We can't find Simon. We need *something*."

She worked her jaw from side to side. Said nothing, just cracked the door and got out. Because he was right.

He met her at the front door of the store where Laney sold books and gifts, as well as local art. She glanced up at him and frowned.

He said, "I'm gonna come inside for a minute." Or, all day.

She pulled the door open, her eyes narrowed in on him again. A bell rang at their entrance, and Laney appeared from the back room. "Drew! I'll get your check."

She disappeared just as fast as she'd appeared.

Ellie turned to him. "Check?"

He nodded. "Laney sells my stuff."

"He's my biggest consignor." Laney strode over, holding out a white envelope. "I'd be sunk if it wasn't for all these North photos. I have stores across the state constantly asking me to reveal how I get them."

Ellie's lips pressed together in a thin line.

Laney's eyebrows rose. "You didn't know." She turned to Drew and gasped. "You didn't tell her? Was it supposed to be a secret?"

Drew didn't answer. He kept his gaze on Ellie. "I'm the photographer, North." His stomach churned. "I changed my last name to Eric and Alma's as soon as I could legally do it. I'm not Drew Turner anymore, even though I use that name with the feds. Legally I'm Andrew North."

Her mouth dropped open. "I didn't even know your *name*?"

"I thought—"

"No." Ellie held up a hand. She strode to the counter and moved behind it. She tugged off her coat. "I can't talk to you right now." Then she disappeared into the back hall.

Laney made a face that pretty much said everything he was thinking. "That didn't go so well."

He shot her a look.

She grinned, but it was short lived. "I had kind of hoped…"

"What?"

"Never mind." She worried her lip. "Keeping that from her wasn't a good idea."

"Because you tell people every secret in the first two days of meeting them?"

He could see from the look on her face that she couldn't argue with that. She sighed. "I should get back to work."

And then he was alone in the storefront. Stood there like a lemon while he wondered what on earth he was supposed to do now. That hadn't gone well at all. *Understatement.* It had been a total train wreck. Drew hadn't exactly thought she would have reacted like that to hearing about his name change.

He sighed, and forced to shift his weight carefully so his knee and hip didn't scream at him. He'd figured she would be able to handle the news. She liked North photographs. Why wouldn't she be pleased it was him? And what was the deal with that name thing?

Drew's phone rang just as he pushed the door open and let himself outside. Cold air brushed at his hair. He pulled out his cell and saw it was Mark calling.

"Morning."

"Not a 'good' one, though?"

Drew said, "If it changes later, I'll keep you posted."

Mark chuckled. "Got a minute?" When Drew said he did, his friend asked, "You know where I can get a photo of Simon Mills?"

"You don't have one?"

"Nothing on the real estate website, license, social media. Nothing."

"That's weird." Didn't real estate agents put their faces on everything? "Maybe I can find one." He turned around on the sidewalk as he thought it through. Maybe Ellie and Laney had a picture of him somewhere, like on their phones. It was possible. "I'll see what I can get, but don't hold your breath."

Through the window he could see them talking. Ellie's

posture was stressed. Hurt. Laney looked like she was trying to reassure her friend.

Drew sighed. Had he messed everything up?

"Did I lose you?"

"No," Drew said. "Anything else?"

"You aren't going to want to hear it."

Drew said, "Whatever it is, just tell me."

"I looked at the medical examiner's report. For your father."

The bottom dropped out of Drew's stomach. "And?"

"Single gunshot wound before he fell off the cliff. The angle is consistent with a suicide." Mark's voice was soft.

"So he wasn't murdered."

"It's still possible—"

"Don't," he said. "Don't worry about it."

What did it matter if his father quit this life instead of sticking around? He'd chosen not to weather the hard times with Drew. At the end of the day his dad had made what he thought was the best decision for himself. Now it was up to Drew to do the same.

Move on. Live the way he wanted—which included having no secrets between him and Ellie. She could react however she wanted, but he'd done nothing wrong in keeping his identity to himself. Taking photos was a huge part of who he was, not just a huge part of his income. He was a private investigator. He knew enough about dirty secrets kept hidden from those who were closest. This was hardly something to make a big deal about in the grand scheme of things. And when she processed her feelings about what she saw as his "deception," she would realize that.

Mark said, "Get me that picture." And hung up.

"Drew!"

He turned to the sound of Laney's call. She waved him

back toward the store. "Coffee will have to wait. Ellie just called in to the sheriff's office."

He stepped inside. "What is it?"

Ellie hung up the phone, her face white. "The receptionist. The sheriff is ruling that Natalie Benson's death was a suicide."

11

She paced across the front of the store, looking at but not seeing any of the books. Figurines. Picture frames. Novelty mugs—she had so many of those at home.

The North photographs.

Laney was looking at her phone to see if she had a picture of Simon Mills. Maybe in the background of some selfie—she took those all the time. Ellie didn't bother looking in hers. She barely took pictures of anything, unless it was so she could reference it later. Like the schedule at work or her dad's shopping list.

"I can't believe he thinks that's going to fly," she said aloud as she moved. "A suicide? That's insane."

There was no way she could stand still right now. Not while this much frustration rolled through her. Not to mention she'd had to choke down a smoothie because swallowing hurt so badly.

"You think he's part of whatever conspiracy is happening in town?"

She swung around to face Drew. "I would've said no. I *would've* said I could trust the sheriff."

"But now you don't?"

"I have no idea." She threw her hands up, then let them fall to her sides. "That's the problem. He let the first shooter go and then those two guys with the knife. They'll probably get a slap on the wrist." Not that such a decision was up to the sheriff. That was the purview of the judge. "Now I have to believe he'll do the right thing with Natalie Benson?"

"You wanna go talk to him, find out why he ruled her death a suicide?" Drew shrugged one shoulder. "I could make my report about last night while we're there."

"You didn't do that yet?"

He shrugged again.

"If I go over there, it'll be by myself. I *don't* need a babysitter."

Laney looked up from her phone and gave her a pointed look. "Ellie."

She blew out a breath. Chastised. She wanted to scream, maybe pull her hair out, and Laney wanted her to remember to be *polite*? This whole situation was enough to make her lose her mind.

If she did that she'd scream at the sheriff, she was so mad. Then she'd get fired. Then she would never figure out what was going on. Drew would get "in" with whoever it was and end up getting killed when they found out he was feeding information back to the FBI. Then where would they be?

She wracked her brain to try and figure out a solution.

"Laney, who owns this store?"

Her friend looked up from her phone, a look on her face Ellie didn't understand. "I do."

Drew tipped his head to the side. "That's unusual, isn't it? I figured you rented."

Something moved over Laney's face. Ellie wasn't sure what it was or why it was directed at Drew. Then she moved it to Ellie. She wanted something from both of them? "What is it?"

Laney looked at her phone. "I'm still trying to find a picture. If I don't have one, I'll check the security video I have for the front door. Maybe he walked past."

Ellie shared a look with Drew. She shrugged. Ellie said, "You own the building?"

Laney said, "That's just how it works in this town. Everyone owns their own property."

"And yet, Northcorp Inland Holdings owns a huge swath of town outside city limits."

Drew nodded. "Literally all the land on the north and west sides of the town."

"So someone is blockading everyone in, making sure the town doesn't spread in that direction?" Ellie asked, even though that was ridiculous. "Getting ready to turn this place into their own stronghold, or something?"

Laney's face paled, but she didn't lift her gaze from her phone.

"I guess that means we need to figure this out." Ellie watched her friend's face while she spoke. "Get to the bottom of it." Like that wasn't painfully obvious considering what was happening, no matter that she and Drew looked like they'd just been through a war.

Laney moved to the computer. It took awhile but they waited. Eventually she came up with a grainy picture of Simon Mills.

Drew had her send a screen grab of the image to him. "I'll forward it to Mark. See what he can get from running the image through the FBI's databases."

"I'm glad to help." She didn't look glad, though. She looked...

Ellie didn't know. She nodded anyway. "Thanks, Laney." She turned to Drew. "I need to go find my father."

He hadn't been answering his phone. That voicemail he'd left her wasn't helpful. She needed to talk to him. Find out what he knew about what was going on in town.

"Good idea." Laney nodded. "I'll be fine here. This is more important than you helping me with inventory."

She was right. There would be time for that later. Some people might think it was strange, but she enjoyed the monotony of it. Checking off a list to marry up inventory counts was something she liked to do. While she was doing it, her subconscious could work on whatever problem—usually a case—was rolling around in her head.

Often, she came up with an answer while doing it. Plus, it helped her friend run her business since she didn't have to do everything herself. And Ellie got a staff discount on mugs.

Drew spoke up. "I'll go with you."

"Because you don't have a ride?" She was still kind of mad he hadn't told her his last name was North now. Or that he was a famous photographer. Maybe not nationally famous, but she knew from Laney that the business she did online, plus foot traffic in the store, was substantial. People visited the town just to come by the store and look at his photos.

His voice was softer when he said, "Let me come with you, Ellie."

Decision time. Did she want him to stick around, considering everything? Yes. He'd been there for her. He'd protected her. Helped her. A sounding board. Was she mad that he hadn't told her all the details of his life? Maybe. It was probably not okay that she was mad. It wasn't like they'd had the chance to share all that much. She certainly hadn't told him everything about her life.

Did she even want to?

Talk about ripping open a wound and letting him take a look. He was going to have an opinion. Or he'd just be sympathetic, and maybe that would be worse. Much worse than finding out he was her favorite photographer.

Ellie nodded. "Fine. Let's go. But only because I want to know the story of how you took that picture." She pointed to her favorite one, hanging on the wall.

Drew actually laughed. "Deal."

It was like a glimmer of good in the middle of everything going on. People trying to kill her. Secrets destroying those who called this town their home. How was she supposed to make sense of all that? And then there was Drew. In the middle of it all, doing his thing. Confident he could handle whatever it was. Get to the bottom of things.

She wanted to believe it. Wanted to trust him. But how did she do that when her faith in people—and God—had been so eroded?

Her dad was AWOL. Even Laney was acting weird.

Ten minutes later they were on the road, headed for her dad's house. Only there was a problem.

"What is it?" He shifted in his seat.

Oh, now he was able to tell that something was wrong? She said, "Someone is following us."

———

DREW LET OUT A FRUSTRATED SOUND. If he turned to look, he would be twisting his hip and his knee. Putting too much pressure on both. Right now he was skimming the edge of his leg giving out altogether. At least so far today. Sitting down was more uncomfortable but also didn't run the risk of him collapsing in front of Ellie.

He slid his gun from its holster under his shoulder.

"Easy there."

"Just in case."

Drew squeezed his teeth together and shifted in his seat

to angle his body toward the door. He could lean out the window if he needed to. But this wasn't the Wild West, and they weren't likely to get in a shootout. He leaned in and looked at the wing mirror.

"You gonna call this in?"

"So Barb can ask me what exactly a suspicious truck looks like?"

"Guess not." Neither of them laughed, though at any other time it would have been a joke. "Keep heading to your dad's."

"Agreed." She took a turn.

Drew had to brace himself. Still, he couldn't hold back the wince. As he shifted in his seat, he focused instead on the truck behind them and less on his own discomfort. She turned another corner. The other vehicle made the same move. Five minutes later, she pulled into her dad's driveway.

Drew was ready with his phone. He shoved the door open and took a burst of pictures. The truck sped past them.

In the driver's seat was a man with dark hair and a beard, holding a pistol up.

He got images of it all.

"Drew."

He turned to look across the roof of the truck, hopping so he didn't twist his leg. "What is—"

The front door was open. She pulled her gun and went first. Drew scanned the street, teeth gritted against the pain in his leg and hip, but he saw no movement. The truck was gone. He headed inside.

The coffee table had been flipped over. A chair from the dining table lay on its side—what was left of it. Pieces of it littered the floor, along with broken glass. A pool of liquid. Coffee, probably.

"Dad!" She called out for him. Raced through the house,

while Drew took a closer look at the living/kitchen area. Open plan. He'd always liked…

There was a trail.

He followed it to the back door, which was ajar. The front had been open. The rear door was only an inch or so cracked.

He pushed it open. "Will!"

No answer.

A plastic patio chair was on its side. Someone had been dragged across the slab of concrete. Blood on the step. Just one spot. Like a blow. He fell, or was dropped.

Drew winced just imagining what that had felt like. Whoever's blood that was likely had a concussion.

He looked back at the house. When had this happened?

Had Ellie's father been attacked, or kidnapped?

Drew called out to him again. Heard the neighbor's dog bark in reply. The yard wasn't big. The rear chain link fence was four feet high.

He scanned it.

His feet were moving before he even realized he'd seen something. Or some*one* lying back there, tucked behind the tree. Discarded.

"Ellie, back here!"

His knees hit the grass. Drew let out a cry of pain as Ellie burst from the back door. She ran over. "What is it?"

He rotated onto the good side of his hip. "Call…ambulance." He could hardly get the words out.

She let out a cry of her own and knelt beside her father. "Dad." She prayed aloud, asking for God to save his life. Drew pulled out his phone and dialed emergency services. He handed her the phone.

"Here." That was all he could get out before rolling away from them in order to deposit his breakfast back up on the grass.

"…*now.*" She hung up. "You okay?"

Drew didn't want to talk about himself. "How is he?"

"It's not good. Looks like he's been beaten. The ambulance should be here in a couple of minutes."

Her father let out a moan. Low and full of pain. Drew didn't like the sound of it at all.

Will's lips parted and a breath escaped. "Ellie."

"I'm here."

"…knew you'd come."

"Of course I came."

It hurt to listen to the old man's voice, especially when he couldn't help much right now.

She said, "That's what we do, right? That's what you told me."

The EMTs came then, and the two of them moved out of the way while they loaded her father onto a backboard.

Drew snagged Ellie's hand because he wanted to hold it. "Let's go."

Ellie nodded. That stark, pain-filled look on her face was there all the way to the hospital. They sat in the waiting room, ready to get word at any moment that they'd stabilized former sheriff Will Maxwell. That he would be all right.

Drew put his arm around her shoulder and tugged her against his side. "He'll be okay." He whispered the words against the skin of her forehead.

"I need to call Laney. I need to—" Her voice broke.

"All that can wait. What's important is that we found him."

"But they hurt him."

He nodded, knowing she would feel the motion against her hair. "I know. But he's alive, right? That's what counts."

"I don't know what I'd do without him."

Drew said, "I don't know what I'd have done without him, either."

She shifted to look at him. "Tell me what you mean."

"He never said anything, past telling me to pack. I knew what'd happened." Drew's breath hitched in his chest. "I *knew* he was gone. Your dad drove me to Eric and Alma North."

"Your family. The people whose name you took."

He nodded. "Alma is a photographer but only for fun. She taught me everything she knew about cameras. About lighting. That's why I changed my name. Part of it, at least." He paused. "She gave me that gift. It's a legacy now, one that has nothing to do with my father."

His heart wanted to break for the pain his dad had been in that led him to take his own life. There was never a way to understand what someone was going through in their own mind.

And you couldn't always know that someone was suffering.

He couldn't say what the right decision would have been, and whether or not it was the one his dad made. What Drew did know was that God had been right there with him the whole time. Through it all, his Heavenly Father had blessed him with everything he needed.

And now He had given Drew another thing. He'd given him Ellie.

Drew's phone started ringing in his pocket right as the doctor strode into the room. "Ellie Maxwell?"

Ellie jumped to stand.

"Your father is asking for you."

She turned back to look at him. "He probably wants to speak to you as well."

"I'll be there in a second." He pulled out his phone and showed her the screen so she'd know he was taking a call.

He swiped the screen, then watched her walk away. "Yes?"

"I ran the picture."

"And?" What had Mark found?

"I better be getting overtime for this or something."

"Sorry."

"It's fine. I told the director what I was doing, and that it was your case. He said take however long it needs."

"He did?"

"I guess you impressed him in Reno."

Drew shook his head. That entire job had been on a knife edge—balanced between success and epic failure. Thankfully God had allowed it to fall toward a good result.

"Tell me what you found."

Mark did. Drew felt his eyebrows rise. He started walking for the room where Ellie had gone. He found her in low conversation with her father.

She started to turn to him. "Wha—"

He hung up the phone. "Simon Mills is a wanted con artist."

12

Ellie took a step back. Her gaze snagged on her father, his purple face. Swollen eyes, cheeks bruised. He had a fractured wrist—suffered when he'd been forced to defend himself—along with three busted ribs. The doctor was worried about internal bleeding.

She turned to him. "You knew?"

He didn't need to answer. The shift of his features was enough to prove his guilt to her.

"Dad, that guy is a criminal."

"Like I don't know that? There just wasn't much I could do about it without everything blowing up. I told the sheriff what I could."

Drew moved closer to the end of the bed. "Did they put pressure on you?"

"That's not a reason to keep something like this a secret." She couldn't believe what she was hearing. Did Drew think what her father had done, keeping it to himself, was acceptable? She swung back to her dad. "I get that you've had a bad day, but we all have." He could tell that from just looking at them.

And only one of them in this room was hooked up to IV pain medication.

"I don't have to explain myself to you."

"I'm not twelve." Like her father didn't know that? "The time to protect me, or talk to me like I'm a child is over."

"I'll always be your father. And until you have children of your own, you'll never understand that."

Hot tears filled her vision. "Nice, Dad. Real nice."

"That was a long time ago, baby girl."

"So I should get over it? Or I should already *be* over it?" She waited for only a split second. A courtesy though, considering she didn't really want an answer. "Why don't you tell me what to feel? Because obviously you *know*."

Drew stood silent. She wanted to explain.

He'd told her about his photographs. Eventually she would tell him about all she'd lost, just not now. This was hardly the time, considering her father was apparently the kind of former sheriff who protected criminals.

She squared her shoulders. "Did you take money from them?"

She needed to know who "they" were, but first she had to ascertain how deeply her father was involved.

"It isn't like that, El."

"Then explain what it is like," she said. "Because you were the sheriff of this county for nearly twenty years. You had to have known someone in this town was buying up property by forcing people out and paying them off. You must know who they are and why they've been doing it."

"Not like its some great conspiracy." He suddenly looked older to her than she'd ever seen him look; he'd always been so full of life. It wasn't just his injuries, though those looked extensive. Maybe fatigue? But there was something about him that was now so...frail. As though life had beaten down on him along with those attacking fists.

"How am I supposed to know that when you never said anything?"

He winced.

Drew said, "Ellie," caution in his tone.

She turned to him. The first man in her life who had felt like a true partner. And yet, he'd hidden things from her as well. While it was hardly the same thing, it still hurt. Her head understood the logic that the two deceptions didn't compare. Drew's was hardly a deception at all. He'd kept something important to him private and when the time came, he'd shared.

She, on the other hand, had overreacted.

Was she overreacting now?

Ellie pushed out a breath.

Drew said, "Will, can you tell us who is involved?"

"I have ideas. What I don't have is evidence." It encouraged her that he at least looked mad about that. Maybe frustrated. He said, "Simon approached Sheriff Burgess a few months back. Told him he was tied up in something and wanted out, but he wouldn't say what it was. First he wanted guaranteed protection. Money. Safe passage out of here."

"He's a conman. He was playing you."

Her dad shot her a look. "Why d'you think we gave him nothing? Not until he offered up actionable evidence, which he did not. When Burgess told me, I had the same reaction. He would just take what we gave him and disappear. We'd be back to square one." He took a breath, offering her a challenge in his expression. "With a theory and nothing to back it up."

"What is that supposed to mean?"

Drew said, "Who attacked you?"

Evidently he wasn't interested in listening to her and her father bicker. What? That was how they communicated. It worked, didn't it?

Her father looked away.

"Dad—"

"There were two of them. Muscled me out of the house, into the yard. I think they were going to take me with them but someone disturbed them. For some reason they took off."

"So it wasn't to send a message." Drew's voice was solid. As though he purposely fought to have no emotional reaction. Because the person they were trying to intimidate was *her*?

She had come to care about him. Could he say the same about her? She wanted to believe it was true, that what she was feeling was mutual. But how could she know? It was scary enough even thinking about laying out her personal side, the stuff she never shared outside her circle of Laney and her dad. But feelings? That was dangerous territory.

Her dad had gone quiet. Drew, too. Ellie said, "We need to know everything you know about them, Dad. It's a poison affecting this town, and it's time it was rooted out and eradicated."

"They're not vermin. They're your neighbors."

"They won't be for much longer if they're hurting people —committing crimes."

His face shifted. "Yeah? It's that black and white?" He sucked in a choppy breath that looked painful. "Right and wrong. Good and evil."

"What's wrong with that?"

"Life isn't that simple, El."

"I know that."

They needed to leave so he could rest. But how, when someone had attacked him and he was lying there hurt? The sob hitched her breath in the middle. Drew came over and stood close. Her dad lifted his hand, a pulse monitor on his finger. She reached out and held his hand.

"I want to know who did this."

"I know you do, but they won't like it. You're already in danger."

He thought she'd be in even more danger? "I don't believe Burgess is innocent. Not for one second do I believe that."

"Then you've already convicted us all, Ellie. You gotta believe we're just trying to make the best of it."

"By allowing people to suffer?"

"It was never supposed to come to this." He used their entwined hands to motion to her and Drew.

"What about the receptionist at the real estate office? She's dead. Burgess ruled it a suicide, but there's no way." She took a breath. "And Drew's father? Did he kill himself, or was he another one of their victims? How long have they been killing people to cover up what they're doing?"

The door shut. Drew was gone.

———

DREW LEANED AGAINST THE WALL, folded forward and hung his head. This was about his knee and his hip. That was what he wanted to believe, at least. It wasn't about the fact she'd voiced what he had been thinking. The truth he'd told himself to believe, instead of the bitter pill of reality.

He repeated to himself what he'd been forced to come to grips with years ago; his father hadn't been taken from this world by someone intent on doing him harm. He'd chosen it.

Drew had to accept that. He couldn't entertain other ideas. If he did, he would mess up all the work he had done to convince himself it had nothing to do with him or whether or not he was worth sticking around for. He had no idea what had gone on in his father's head. And he never would.

What he had to do now was keep putting one painful foot

in front of the other. Keep moving. Live his life. Be the best he could be, regardless of what anyone else thought.

Was that why he'd been determined to think the town would never understand him? Maybe it was safer to assume they'd never take the time to get to know who he really was.

He blew out a breath and straightened. That was when she left her father's room.

"I'm sorry." The question was there on her face. "What did I say?"

Drew didn't want her to feel bad. She had enough going on without him adding to it, but he wasn't going to lie to her either. "My father." He pushed out a breath. "I don't think he was murdered. But it just hit me, how you said it. Made me realize how much I wanted it to be true." He tried to smile. Brush it off.

Her eyes filled with tears. "I'm sorry."

He pulled her to him. "Don't worry about it. I'm glad your father is okay."

She pulled back, making a face. "Maybe. He told me they approached him years ago about 'investing in the community.' He saw it for what it was and told them to go shove it. Figured it wouldn't be long before he was in their pocket."

She shook her head and continued, "But if he wasn't fighting them, maybe he was helping them in a way. Keeping his head down. Pretending nothing was wrong. On any other day he's being complicit in what they're doing."

"What about him working with Sheriff Burgess to get some evidence?" That was what Will had told them. That both the current sheriff and the previous sheriff were actively looking for evidence on this case. They wanted the people forcing others from their homes to be stopped.

"He doesn't even know who the players are." She stepped

back and folded her arms. "It could be anyone in town for all we know."

"Except the man who spoke to me in the hospital room."

"So we get the security footage?"

Drew had been thinking the same thing. "Get a face, figure out who the mastermind is."

"And if he's from out of town like Simon Mills? Someone with an untraceable ID that we can't find, can't pin anything on."

He blew out a breath. "Simon Mills is wanted. So I know it looks impossible. They've been hiding their activities and their identities for years. But they've messed up this week. They came after you. They even hired men to do it. Then there's the guy who strangled you." He had to swallow that down. "That means they're stressed. And stressed people mess up. They get sloppy. So we go talk to the bank manager. The mayor. People in the land office, just like Laney suggested. See what shakes loose."

She nodded. "If I go in there, they'll know I'm asking in an official capacity."

No one in town was under any misconception that Ellie was 100 percent about the job. That level of focus was impressive. He did the same thing when he was undercover, going all in until the task was complete.

This time it was far more personal.

In more ways than one.

"So I go in," he said. "You listen from outside. I'll wear a wire, and we can get it all on tape." Not his usual mode of operating, but he highly doubted the locals here would be worried about checking him for a listening device. He wouldn't wear one for a meet. That was too dangerous. Just for poking around, asking a few questions.

"Okay." She nodded.

Just like that. One suggestion, and she didn't even raise

any objections. He was honestly surprised Ellie would be okay sending him in when she was usually so take-charge. But she was right. She had her skill set, and he had his.

"Stay with your dad for right now. I need to go get some things."

Her eyes widened. "You think someone might approach him like they did with you. You think they might even try to kill him again?" She let out a frustrated noise. "I've been trying to convince myself that I don't have anything to worry about."

"Sorry," he said. "Maybe you should call Burgess, ask him to come sit with your father. Or Laney. Or someone else you trust."

"Laney won't be much in the way of protection. She's a shop owner, and I'm not sure she's ever had to defend herself in her entire life." Ellie shot him a wry smile. "Though, that's not a bad thing."

"She might not be trained, but someone looking to come here and cause trouble will think twice if they see another person in the room."

"Good thinking."

Drew looked at his watch. "It's pretty late. The city offices and the bank aren't going to be open. We can meet up in the morning and get set up for some surveillance. Are you going to stay here tonight?"

She nodded. "But I'll call Laney. See if she can come here in the morning and sit with him. They don't always get along perfectly, but I'm sure they'll put that aside for the sake of all that is happening."

A loud alarm sounded through speakers, high in the walls. A recorded voice—the same one that announced a color code causing nurses and doctors to spring from their chairs. Drew watched as they ran toward patient rooms. And not just one. "What is it?"

Ellie had already pulled her pistol from its holster. "Threat. Someone alerted security that there's an active shooter in the hospital."

A nurse raced around the corner, headed right toward them. She saw Ellie's weapon and then Drew's, threw her hands up and screamed.

"Sheriff's department," Ellie called out to her. "What's going on?"

The woman kept screaming. She raced past them into a room off the hall.

Drew moved to the desk and spoke to the nurse. "What's happening?"

She had her phone out and her attention on the screen as she tapped and swiped. Then she put the phone to her ear. "Hello?" Her wide, fearful eyes lifted to his and she shoved the chair back as she said into the phone, "There's a gunman in the hospital. I'm so scared."

Drew said, "Stay here." Even though she was talking to someone else. "Get under the desk."

"Let's find the stairs."

He followed Ellie to the stairwell door. "Why don't you stay with your dad? I can see what's going on." He patted the pocket where his phone was. "I'll call."

She was torn. He could see it on her face. He said, "It's okay to stay up here. We don't even know what's happening. Could be nothing."

"Really?" Another facial expression he could read well. She didn't believe it any more than he did.

"There's a chance."

Just like there was a chance that someone was here to kill her father. Or him. Or her. Or all of them.

Footsteps pounded up the stairs. Drew hit the bar and the door cracked open. The sound got way louder. He listened for any talking, wanting to know if this was friend or foe.

If someone was here to kill her father, they might not even know that Drew and Ellie were on the same floor.

A security guard came into view, huffing from his sprint up the stairs. His eyes widened at the sight of both of them, guns out.

Ellie pulled a leather wallet from her back pocket.

The man sighed. "Guess that makes you the one in charge, Deputy."

He lifted his gun and fired at Ellie. A boom that echoed in the concrete stairwell.

Before either of them could react, she fell back.

13

Ellie's world went dark for a second. She heard the deafening rap of another gunshot, only a split second after the first one. Fighting the black of unconsciousness, she blinked her eyes open.

The security guard hit the floor, leaving only Drew standing. Gun pointed at the spot where the man had been.

"Ellie!" He crouched, their eyes meeting.

She blinked.

"You gotta breathe, Ellie."

Why was he…

She sucked in a lungful of air.

"There you go."

He tugged her shirt from her waistband. "You're wearing a vest." In one move, buttons went flying and her body was jerked. "It saved your life."

"Hurts though." That was all she could say. Her chest felt like she'd been punched by a freight train. She touched the spot and found the crumpled remnants of what had been a round. A bullet that would have killed her had she not been wearing a vest.

She'd only taken it off to sleep the past few days. And often wore it on her days off, considering how many times her dad had been shot in the twenty years he was a sheriff. There was just no way to account for the exact moment of a surprise attack.

Only the ability to minimize the damage when it *did* come.

Because trouble would come. She was certain of it, and she'd been right. Satisfaction didn't make it hurt less, though. She hissed out a breath.

"Let's get you help." He moved to lift her in his arms, then shifted. Tugged her arm over his shoulder. "You're gonna have to help me or I'll wind up lying here with you after my knee gives out."

She got her feet under her.

"Good."

They stumbled to the desk, and he got on the phone. She laid her head forward, down on the bar-height counter to listen to him tell whoever was on the other end that he had a gunman up here, dead.

A security guard.

Or a man dressed as one?

She wanted to go back and see if he'd forgotten to leave his wallet at home. Maybe he'd even called in the shooter threat to distract everyone while he came upstairs to kill them.

She lifted her head and straightened, unable to bite back the moan. Drew caught her elbow, and she went with him to the door of her father's room.

Her dad was sitting up. "Someone came here?"

Drew said, "He shot Ellie. I killed him."

Her dad's head whipped to her, shirt still open and the bullet lodged in her vest on full display. "Too soon to say I told you so?"

"Yes. But you don't need to, because I took your advice. If I hadn't, I would be dead."

Her dad nodded. "Exactly."

Ellie wanted to fight more with him. The kind of fighting they did was cathartic, letting out their emotions in a controlled way, knowing neither cared what was said. They still loved each other. No, it wasn't a normal father/daughter relationship. But it was theirs, and they made it work.

"Who was he?"

"Dressed as a security guard." Drew handed his phone to her dad. "Recognize him?"

He'd taken a picture? She studied her dad's grizzled features for a reaction. His gaze slid over her before he met Drew's. "No idea."

What that meant, she didn't know. "We need information, Dad. Who hurt you? Who are these people? Now isn't the time to hold back what you know. I could be lying back there. Dead." She waved toward the hall and the stairwell. Too much movement. Pain swelled in her. She fought the tide of it, not wanting to succumb.

She'd done that before. Given in when life got too overwhelming. This time it was all physical, whereas before it had been a combination of physical and emotional. Grief. Pain. Loss. This was a fight for survival just like that, a battle to keep putting one foot in front of the other.

Was that why she was so drawn to Drew? He too had suffered so much. He knew what loss was. To have to let go of the person who was closest to you. His relationship with his father wasn't something she knew much about, but he had loved and lost. In whatever way that came.

She had, as well. Though only for a short time. The weeks in-between taking that test in the bathroom of her college dorm and telling her boyfriend. Their hasty marriage at the courthouse.

And what had happened only weeks later.

All of it years ago now, but she could still remember every second in high-definition detail.

"Ellie." His voice came from far away.

She realized she was lying on a bed in a room that was empty except the two of them. She must have passed out. "I'm okay."

His thumb swiped across her cheek. "You're crying."

She was. Ellie didn't know what to say. Part of her wanted to apologize, but she realized that wasn't what she needed to say. He knew. He'd felt grief. Not the same way. But he knew. "What happened?"

"You passed out. I had the doctor take a look at you." His face was soft. She tried to sit up, and he helped her. She felt better. But fuzzy. "Pain meds?"

"He did an X-ray. You didn't break anything."

She nodded. Drew must have seen something in her eyes. He backed up. "The sheriff is here."

Ellie forced her pained body from the room while he held her hand in his warm, strong one. The vest had been removed, and she hadn't been changed into a gown. What a nightmare that would've been. The fact they'd wheeled her around and poked her with a needle, taken an X-ray, all while she'd been unconscious was bad enough.

At the doorway, she squeezed his hand. A signal to let go.

He did, a smile curving the corners of his lips, holding the phone to his ear. She liked that he was so readily able to smile. He whispered, "Go."

She moved first, heading straight for the sheriff.

When she neared, Drew said, "Gotta go," into his phone, then hung up and glanced at her as they walked. "You okay?"

She said, "Mostly." Because she made a point never to lie to him. "Though I could use a chair."

He led the way to a waiting area and sat beside her, the sheriff opposite. He leaned his elbows on his knees. "Your dad is okay as well?"

She nodded.

Drew said, "No one was hurt, right?"

"Right." The sheriff shifted one knee. Nervous?

"We know you're looking for a way to bring them down." She didn't want to give him much in the way of concessions. She'd been on this case for maybe a couple of weeks before she'd approached Drew—no thanks to the sheriff telling her to leave it alone. Now she knew why, and she had the marks and bruises to show for it. And a knife wound. A bruise from a bullet.

"Every time I think I get near something, there's nothing there." His earnest eyes met hers.

"I wanna close in. I just need a direction to aim. Someone I can roust out of bed right now to get some answers." She laid a hand over the bruise. "Enough is enough, Burgess. This needs to be finished."

"You get to the bottom of it, and I'll make sure the full weight of the law comes down on them." He sat back and nodded. "It's time we got this town back."

Ellie was all for that. But a tiny voice at the back of her mind wanted an answer to one question.

How much more would victory cost them?

———

To her credit, Ellie hid most of her surprise. The sheriff still spotted her reaction though. He stared at her for a while. Absorbed the weight of her opinion of him, and taking it on board.

"I'm not the man you seem to think I am. I want justice done." He ran a hand along his jaw. "Every time I think I'm close to finding something that would get me a warrant, or at least something that could lead to more…" He blew out a breath. "I get fifty times the pushback. To the point that even thinking about putting my career and my life on the line makes me feel like I've been hit by a cattle prod."

Ellie said nothing. Processing his words through the fog. She wasn't doing well at all, and her brain was likely hazy from the pain meds he'd had them dose her with before she woke up. It wasn't like she would have taken any pills. In the end, he'd had her father sign off on it.

The doctor hadn't been under any illusion that they were taking her choice away. But it was for the best. She couldn't fight this through sheer strength of will. And she wouldn't do herself any favors if she tried.

He said, "It's good to know where you stand. That you *do* want this taken care of."

"We all do." Ellie's voice was soft with the effects of the medicine, but he could hear the streak of tension there. "That's not in question. If it were, we'd be having a different conversation right now. One where I'd be asking you to honestly rethink your hold on that badge." She motioned to it, pinned to the man's shirt.

"I'm thinking about that anyway," he said. "Considering what future I have if I let this go on. I'm wondering if bringing this to a close might not be the last thing I do before I move on to retirement."

Drew glanced at Ellie. Would she be after the sheriff's job? It was an elected position but from the sense he got around town, people would likely vote her in. Maybe only for the fact she was a "known" versus an "unknown." They'd know what they were getting with her in the boss's chair.

She definitely had *his* vote.

Ellie would make an excellent sheriff. She would do a great job at a bunch of other things as well. The protective streak in her would make her the best kind of mother. And as a wife, he'd never have to worry. She could take care of herself.

The fact he was even thinking about that meant he needed to check himself. Drew could hardly drag a woman and a relationship into the life he led. His career took him all over and at any moment that could mean the difference between life and death. No one—not just Ellie—would want to be saddled with that.

After all, he was hardly in town but maybe a few days every month. The rest of the time he wasn't exactly in a place where he could have regular long phone conversations, or often even get away to reply to a text. That would get old pretty fast.

He didn't want to treat the woman he fell in love with that way.

The sheriff stood, slapped his hat against his thigh and set it on his head. "If you wanna rouse someone out of bed, I suggest you take a look at Barb."

Ellie gaped. "Your *dispatcher*?"

His stubble-covered jaw shifted. "Only thing that makes sense to me is that she's their eyes and ears in the office. No other way they could know what they know."

She blew out a breath. "Wow."

Drew didn't disagree. "You really think they put a plant in your department?"

"And that it isn't Coughlan." Ellie folded her arms.

The sheriff said, "That's who would be your guess?"

"Honestly, my guess was you."

"I know." His eyes flashed hurt, despite his words. Drew figured the sheriff knew he'd earned that from her. Distrust and suspicion were going to be hard to shake. "But I'm telling you, look at Barb."

Ellie watched him leave.

"What do you think?" He held out his hand and helped her to her feet.

She sighed. "I think he should have done this years ago. Before it got this bad."

"Twenty-twenty hindsight?"

"I don't have that luxury," she said. "I'm in the middle of this, and it's happening *now*."

She said goodbye to her father and made sure the sheriff had someone watching the room. In the end, her boss promised to take care of it himself. Drew watched the disagreement war across her face.

As soon as they left the front doors of the hospital, he called Mark and asked for someone federal to come stand as protection over Will Maxwell. Turned out he knew of an agent on assignment in the area. A man Drew knew as well, from the Northwest Counter Terrorism Taskforce. Mark was going to have the guy—a US marshal, Salvador Alvarez— head over now, since nothing was happening on his other case.

When he told her, the look on Ellie's face was far more rewarding than the cost of him calling in another favor.

Would this be over before he ran out?

She sat with her eyes closed while he drove. Thankfully his swollen knee was on the left, so he could still drive. It was wrapped. The damage wasn't permanent. Like Ellie, he would heal.

Could the town say the same thing?

He pulled up across the other side of the street where Barb lived, able to see the house but not so close she'd see them if she looked out the window. Night air moved the trees. They swayed back and forth, shifting leaves down the middle of the street like a child's game where balls collide against each other.

The sheriff's department receptionist owned a white

compact car. It was parked in the driveway. Had this been any other job, he'd have snuck over there and felt the hood to see how long she'd been home. Then he would creep around the house to get a look inside to see what she was up to.

Working with Ellie wasn't a chore. He had to work within the boundaries of the law either way. But there were definitely fewer restrictions on him—or at least that was the understanding he had with Mark's boss.

Ellie's soft snores filled the cab. He glanced over for a second. She didn't look comfortable, but sleep was healing. He wasn't going to wake her up. At least, he hadn't planned on it.

Until he saw movement.

Drew squeezed her knee and turned on the engine. She came awake along with the car. They could follow a certain distance, but eventually they'd be seen and they'd have to switch to pursuing Barb on foot.

Ellie shifted in her seat and let out a moan.

"Sorry." He didn't like that she was hurting.

"What is it?"

He waited until Barb turned the corner, and then he pulled out. She'd been glancing around. Scurrying on her black shoes along the sidewalk like she didn't want to be seen.

"She's on the move. And she wants to keep it a secret."

"Going to meet someone?"

Drew said, "Let's follow her and find out."

14

Ellie's heart squeezed as they drove after her. Actually, it felt more like it did a flip in her chest. How could Barb betray them all this way? How could she willingly work with whoever was intimidating people? It was possible she'd been pressured. Coerced into helping them by spying on the sheriff's department she'd faithfully served for almost as long as Ellie had been alive.

Yes, that had to be it.

Drew said, "He could be mistaken."

"If he is," Ellie said, "then we should never have left my father at the hospital. Not even for one second, and not even with the protection he has."

"They don't have *everyone* on their payroll." Drew turned a corner, the truck crawling. Keeping a good distance behind Barb. "That isn't possible. You and I would both have realized something was wrong long before this if that were the case."

His voice was as dark as the cab of the truck. He'd turned the headlights off. A natural move, as though he was accustomed to this kind of clandestine operation.

Which of course, he was. Ellie was the one out of her element.

Not much call for surveillance in such a small town. The receptionist's murder was the only one they'd had in Malvern County in nearly six years—and it had been ruled a suicide.

She wanted to go into the office and pull up case files for all the deaths in the county over that amount of time. See if there were any inconsistencies, any "accidental" rulings that could be anything but. Maybe the sheriff had been covering for them this whole time.

And her father's part in it all? She wanted to believe Drew's father hadn't chosen to leave him. But if that was the truth of what had happened, then that meant her own father had suppressed evidence. Betrayed the oath he'd sworn to uphold the law.

Drew turned a corner, still following Barb. She was striding down the sidewalk at a pretty fast clip. She had told Ellie many times about her morning power walks. This wasn't what Ellie had been thinking of. It was after midnight, so technically she supposed it was "morning."

How long could they go before Barb heard the car and they had to pass her to convince her they weren't following? Maybe she was focused and wouldn't notice. But even that wouldn't last much longer.

"So you think the sheriff is in on this?"

Ellie bit her lip. "I don't think it's all or nothing." She remembered her dad's words about gray areas. She'd have condemned any of them—all of them—for taking part in any bit of it, but she didn't know the facts. She didn't know what had been done to them. The ways they had suffered.

She'd thought she was alone in her pain. Instead, the truth was that every one of them had been suffering. Ellie had been so blinded by her own problems, that she hadn't seen it. She'd probably been a horrible friend and knew she'd been a horrible daughter. It was a wonder any of them had given her any kind of acceptance or love. She certainly hadn't deserved it.

She fought through the cloud to say, "I would be more worried about my dad if he hadn't mentioned the sheriff before I did. He's the one who told us Burgess was being leaned on. Forced to comply, or at least stay quiet. And if I hadn't given my dad my backup weapon."

Drew's head whipped around. "You gave a man on pain meds a loaded gun?"

"It's his." Obviously she'd given it to him. He needed to protect himself when she couldn't be there. She said, "What?"

Drew pushed out a heavy breath and went to say something but hesitated and pulled out his phone instead. "Text," he said. "My guy Alvarez is there. The sheriff left when he showed up. After he checked the guy's credentials."

Ellie's eyes were on Barb but she nodded, wondering where the sheriff left to go to. Back to the office? Or somewhere else…like the same place he'd effectively sent them. To where Barb was headed.

His foot tapped the brake, and he pulled to the curb. "She turned a corner."

Whether this was a trap or not, did it matter? Either way, they would get answers. Her dad would be safe. This would be done. Frustration welled up in her. "Let's go."

He laid a hand on her arm. "We can't rush. We have to follow her in a way she doesn't see us."

"And you're the pro at this?" Maybe she hadn't given him any indication that she knew how to follow. Or that she could do it as well as she led.

"Ellie."

"Go." This was important. She wasn't going to do something that messed things up. "I'll be right behind you."

He shut the door on his side quietly. Ellie pulled back right before she slammed it and did the same. She slid her weapon from its holster and checked it. Loaded. Safety on.

Drew glanced once at her, and they crossed the street. His steps were almost silent. She felt like a trainee officer behind him, even though she had years of service under her belt. That was the difference between a small county sheriff's department and federal agencies. Private security and investigations, and local crime. Big city problems bled through here. But it was different.

She wanted to thank him for coming. For being here with her, supporting her in a way no one else was doing. Or had ever done.

And maybe that was because she'd never let them. She hadn't even let God comfort her. She'd just gotten angry and walked away from everything she'd believed. Everything she had leaned on after her mother died. What she'd given up after college. Faith was like this on-again/off-again thing she couldn't seem to get traction on.

They raced to catch up.

At the end of the alley, Barb turned the corner toward the elementary school.

This time of night the place would be locked. Was that where she was going, or was Barb headed somewhere else? Cold moved through her as she contemplated—again—the idea this was a trap. At the end of the day, though, she'd rather it was her and Drew than anyone else in danger. They made a good team. A great team, actually.

Whatever happened tonight, they would face it together.

He slowed at the end of the alley and put his back to the wall, then turned to look around the corner. She watched him until she was sure he'd absorbed everything, then took a second to say, "Thank you."

He didn't move. Didn't turn to acknowledge her words.

Just said, "You're welcome," in a low voice. Soft with the comfort of knowing they were together. Neither of them wanting to do this alone. "She's going into the school." He scanned all directions.

Ellie checked the alley behind them. "We're clear to follow?"

"She has a key."

And when she let go of the door to walk down the hallway, Barb was going to let it click shut behind her. The door would be locked again. There would be no way into the school without breaking a window or door in, and setting off some kind of alarm.

Drew evidently realized the same thing—they'd both gone to school here. He dashed out and raced for the school.

Ellie lifted her weapon and scanned. She would provide cover, since he was completely exposed out there running for the entrance Barb had used.

She saw no one.

Drew grabbed the door at the last second, before it closed. He stood beside it with his hand between the door and the frame.

She hoped Barb didn't look back. Or go back to check and see if the door had properly latched.

For the first time in a long time, Ellie prayed.

———

THEY WALKED the halls of the elementary school together. Ready to face the threat together. Drew knew she felt it too. Why else would she have thanked him, except for the fact they were both here? He'd never had a partner before. This kind of support felt nice.

Only, would it feel like this if it were anyone else here with him? Drew wasn't sure it would.

Still, his thoughts roiled. Better than acknowledging how much it hurt to run.

It had occurred to him that her father may have simply felt guilty for his involvement in what happened to Drew's dad. Or what he'd done. Murder or suicide, Will Maxwell felt the impact of the death of one of the citizens of Malvern County. And possibly his culpability—to whatever extent that reached.

He'd helped Drew that night out of guilt, probably. Maybe that was the only reason he'd done it. Sure, Drew's life had been better as a result. *Infinitely* better, in fact, after he'd gone to live with Eric and Alma. If he was given the opportunity, Drew would thank the man for arranging it. So he had to face the fact that it was a good thing. Despite the reason behind it.

Realizing the man hadn't done it just to help, but also because he'd caused it in part…

Drew blew out a breath and forced his mind to focus on what was happening right now; Barb and the school. A meeting. A trap. Either way, he needed his full attention on this and not on a conversation he could have later.

He took a breath, feeling the restrictions of the protective vest he wore. After Ellie had been shot, he'd put his on. She'd switched hers out for another he had, a spare that was far too big for her, but she'd cinched it all the way tight. Once a vest had been impacted with a bullet, it lost its efficacy. A fact, but a sober one that meant one of them had been shot already today.

God, protect us. Keep us safe so we can unravel this.

He'd prayed many times during operations. Sometimes God was the only "good" he got to talk to, mired in the dark underbelly of society most people never saw. It hardly surprised him that even his home town had a shadowy side —people manipulating others for their own gain.

Help us bring it all to light.

That was his job. To wade into the darkness, grab hold of it and haul it back out to face the light. He had skills. He had training. He had experience. But it was God who brought the victory every time. It was God who shored up the places he was weak and gave him the grace to facilitate justice in the world.

Barb had disappeared into the gym, one that doubled as a lunchroom. This was a small school despite it being the only one in the county. Kids were bussed in from all over Malvern to come here. And they never even knew that this place, which should be safe for them to come and learn, was being used for something entirely more sinister.

The realization moved through him at the same time Ellie tapped his shoulder. He stepped to the side with her, and he saw what she meant. The classroom. When the divider was open, it was the stage in the auditorium. When the divider was closed, it was a classroom.

They snuck in. It was pitch black except for a security light, high on the wall. The exit sign at the other end. Without that, he'd have tripped over a chair. And that pile of books.

Ellie shifted between two music stands, turning sideways. The way she moved was like a dance. He could have watched her all day. But that attraction wasn't going to help here. And neither would it aid in his resolve.

Though, if he were honest, that was rapidly disintegrating. He wanted her in his life. Partners. The full, God-given, realization of what that meant.

Another conversation for later, considering where they were—and the fact he'd hesitated to bring a woman into the life he lived. On the road for weeks on end. Constant danger. Keeping secrets because he'd signed non-disclosure agreements.

They crept to the divider, a partition that could be slid back. Probably the same one that had hung here back when he and Ellie went to school.

Ellie knelt at the side, all the way to the left, and peered through the gap between the divider and the wall. Drew looked above her, shifting his weight to take the pressure off his screaming knee. The floor in the auditorium was four feet below the stage and stretched out to the basketball hoop at the other end.

In the center, a group of people were gathered. They were too far away for Drew to hear what was being said, but given the gesturing, he'd say there was some dissension in the group. One man wasn't happy. Barb tried to reassure him, but he shook his head. Wouldn't listen. Deputy Coughlan stood at the edge of the gathering, arms crossed.

He could hear each intake of Ellie's breath, along with his own as they watched. Waited. But then she wasn't just breathing. She gasped. Her whisper hit his ears. "Laney."

Drew found her among the group. Ellie's best friend was here, among the six people gathered.

She was one of them.

Drew could hardly believe it. He reached down and set his hand on her shoulder. There was nothing he could say, not without being heard. She'd already risked their lives whispering her friend's name.

The door at the end flung open.

He squeezed Ellie's shoulder and then let go. Laney. Barb. The other three, apart from the sheriff's deputy, were men of differing ages, but he couldn't be sure who they were. The biggest realization was that the sheriff wasn't among them.

Two more men entered, rough looking guys. Could be the two men with the truck who'd been paid to hurt Ellie, but he'd thought they were in custody. They dragged another man between them. He hung limp in their grasp, and Drew thought he might have caught blood dripping on the floor.

They let go of him in the center of the group, and the man hit the floor. He groaned.

Still alive, then.

More arguing began, some loud enough he could hear the words echo to them.

"…to do!"

"…out of control!"

Laney and Barb were about as happy as the men. Drew tried to gauge who was in charge from their body language, but couldn't tell. Maybe the man to the left. Older, wearing a suit. Or was it just the arrogance in his bearing that made Drew think that? He couldn't be sure.

Neither could he be sure who the guy was. He knew what the mayor looked like and didn't think he was here. He'd never met the rest—the bank manager and other county employees who Laney, of all people, had suggested as candidates. He didn't know what they looked like. Maybe Ellie could ID the players here.

Things weren't going the way the group wanted them to. Too much attention being drawn to them? Too much heat from Ellie that they hadn't dealt with. She wasn't going to accept being silenced.

Laney knew that.

And if she'd told them, their only conclusion would be that Ellie had to be silenced *permanently.*

The suited guy strode to the downed man and used a grip on his hair to lift the man's head. Simon Mills. He was here, and he'd been beaten before he was dragged in. His hands were bound, not that he looked to be in any position to put up a fight.

Whatever agreement the conman had drawn up with this group, they weren't satisfied. Maybe he'd taken steps to double cross them, rob them. That kind of stuff happened when someone got into business with a person whose livelihood came from defrauding people. Deceiving them.

He wouldn't be doing that much longer.

The suited man drew a gun from the back of his belt and shot Simon Mills.

15

Ellie forced away all thoughts but the ones that were a part of her training. This couldn't be personal, or it would never be over. *Laney is one of them.* Now wasn't the time to let that paralyze her.

She pulled out her phone. They'd just shot someone.

Correction: Alan Franz, the bank manager, had shot Simon Mills.

Ellie made sure her silent phone didn't have the flash on and pulled up her camera. She took a handful of photos. The group. The body.

The people in the room—she couldn't think about the fact she knew them—started to dissipate. The men who'd hauled Simon Mills in picked him up again. There would be physical evidence here, no matter how well they tried to clean up. Under the surface there would be proof to find. And now she knew exactly where to look.

Exactly who the targets of her investigation were going to be.

Drew squeezed her shoulder again.

She turned to him. What could be said? They didn't want to give away their position. Too many people in that room meant they would be seriously outnumbered in an arrest. Would the group cut and run, leaving the slowest behind? They would end up with only low-hanging fruit.

This had to stay reconnaissance if they wanted to keep from being overpowered. If they wanted to gain the chance to get the whole group later. Those who escaped today could go to ground. They might never find them if there were escape plans in place.

Ellie had no idea if they were prepared and ready to get away. Allowing them to escape the consequences was the last thing she wanted. Instead, they had to make sure every one of these people found themselves in handcuffs.

Even Laney.

A sob worked its way up her throat, but she swallowed it back down. *Don't let me give in.* Ellie pulled up her texts and sent all the photos to the sheriff, along with a quick explanation of what had happened. He sent them here, and it hadn't been a trap.

Drew squeezed her elbow and motioned to the door. He mouthed, *Come on.*

She nodded and followed him, watching her phone's indicator to see when her messages were read. Drew tugged her around obstacles. Neither of them wanted to hang around and be sitting ducks.

At the door she stowed her phone so no one could see the light. They stepped into the hallway.

Halfway across, headed for the exit, the side door to the auditorium opened. A man she'd seen at church, but whose name she didn't know, stepped out, followed by someone else. Ellie didn't wait around to see who it was.

"Run!" She shoved at Drew, and they sprinted forward.

Her body was a mass of aches and pains, and fatigue, but she pushed all that aside.

Footsteps, ones that spanned the end of the hall, followed them.

Shots rang out.

Ellie ducked her head. Instinct pushed her to press against the wall and make a smaller target out of her body. Drew swerved into her, then tugged her left, forcing her to change direction. He turned his body at the last second and hit the exit bar with his palm. With his right hand, he lifted a gun and fired off two shots.

Ellie ducked between him and the door and cut right to find cover behind the other door. She fired two shots of her own back down the hallway while Drew stepped out and got out of the line of fire.

He grabbed her free hand, and they ran. Ellie focused on breathing and getting her legs to keep moving. His breath was sharp and fast beside her. She listened to it and the pounding of their feet on the blacktop of the playground.

Over the gate. Down the little alley between houses. Across the cul-de-sac to the street where he'd left the truck.

She didn't let any other thought creep in until she reached the truck. She should call in shots fired. She should call in the meeting and update the sheriff on what they'd seen. But she didn't. They needed to regroup. Make a plan where they tracked down the group's members one by one. With enough personnel, they'd get it done fast. Hopefully as close to simultaneous as they could.

Ellie dialed the sheriff's number. He answered with a short, "Ellie?"

She sucked in breaths and tried to explain in broken words and phrases what had happened.

"Do you want me to come to you?"

"Tell him no." Drew pulled the truck door open and

shoved her inside. "Go. Get across." He glanced back at the alley, like he was waiting for a gunman to show up any second now.

She climbed in, groaning at the feel of that gunshot bruise in her chest.

Drew got in behind her. He took the phone, maybe seeing that she wasn't going to be able to think this through right now. "Yeah. You got the photos?" He paused, listening. "Copy that. I'll keep you posted."

He hung up, already pulling out.

"What did he—"

"We're going to meet him first thing. Tonight, we lay low. He's going to the judge to get warrants so we can dig up these guys from whatever holes they crawl into."

That meant Laney, too.

"And he's going to call Mark. Get some help."

She wanted to say something. Tried.

Drew squeezed her knee and then grabbed the wheel again with both hands as he hit the gas and headed for the highway. "Right now, all we're going to do is hunker down and pray we didn't stir up the hornet's nest." He didn't sound happy. "He *had* to know what we were walking into, but he said nothing. He sent us after Barb, on a wild goose chase that led to murder." He blew out a breath and gripped the steering wheel with both hands. "Now we just have to stay alive long enough to testify to it."

Ellie blinked.

"You should buckle your seatbelt."

She did as he asked. Teeth gritted. Then Ellie shut her eyes. Her breath stuttered mid-inhale. His hand squeezed her knee. She wanted to curl up in a ball and cry. Then sleep for a week. She couldn't even think about telling Drew about that worst time in her life.

Would they ever get the chance?

"It's going to be okay, Ellie. I know it doesn't seem like that right now. But it will. I promise."

She felt the tear roll down her cheek and didn't bother to swipe it away. Laney had been her best friend since Kindergarten. Even through the separation of college, her friend had been there for her. They'd visited often. Talked on the phone all the time.

Laney knew everything about her. Every sordid thing she'd ever done wrong, she'd confessed it all to her friend. Certain that her sounding board would love her, no matter what. Now she knew it was nothing but lies. Ellie had leaned on her for support, but her friend hadn't done the same. Laney had been pulled into something serious, with bad people and broken laws. She'd said nothing. She'd given them no indication that she'd known exactly what they were walking into.

And when Alan Franz had pulled that trigger, she'd just stood there like it was no big deal.

Now Ellie was sitting here in Drew's truck while the fabric of her life unraveled.

———

HE GRIPPED THE PHONE. "No, she's not okay. And I think we have a tail."

Mark said, "Can you lose them?"

"There's nowhere to go." And neither of them were in a position to get out and hike for hours. They'd been driving for miles, doing circles around the town until it was safe to find a place to lie low. They'd get back to his cabin at some point but would they even be protected there? "I can try and outrun them. I don't know what else to do."

"I'm about two hours out of town."

"I thought the assistant director was sending a team?"

"There was a threat made to the college. He reassigned everyone except me and Brian." That was the guy who'd been sitting with Will Maxwell for hours, debriefing him about this whole mess. Protecting Ellie's father while the two of them tried to chase down Barb.

And what a can of worms that had turned out to be.

Drew sighed.

"Listen, I know it's not ideal…"

He didn't need Mark apologizing. "Don't worry about it. We'll figure it out."

Drew took a sharp turn. Ellie's head lolled against the window. Passed out, or dozing and half asleep. He figured her body had shut down after being pushed way too hard and way too far. He couldn't carry her. Not with his knee like this. He was close to the breaking point himself.

"I gotta make another call."

"Okay." Mark hung up, no questions asked.

Drew was glad for it. He needed to get on with this if he was going to get Ellie out of here and lose the person following them. They were hanging back, far enough he wasn't completely convinced they were in pursuit. But something about it just didn't sit right. Would it turn aggressive before he could get his plan in place?

Ten minutes to get there.

Ellie's phone started to ring. He could hear the vibration against the sides of the cup holder he'd shoved it in. She roused, pulling it out so she could look at it. "Laney." Her voice was thick with sleep, though he didn't think she'd been completely out.

Drew took the phone. "Don't answer it."

Were they being tracked? Laney could be calling just to talk to her friend. She could also be calling for any number of other nefarious reasons.

"Drew—"

He hit the button on his door panel. The window started to whir down and he tossed the phone out.

"What are you—"

"Stop screaming." His head already hurt. And if she gave in, combatting the grief of betrayal by screaming, she would only feel worse afterwards. "Yes, your friend betrayed you. I'm sorry." He took a breath. "You have no idea how sorry I am about that. But it's done." He wanted to know how he, with all his instincts from undercover work, hadn't even realized who Laney really was.

"The photos I took were on that phone!"

Drew gritted his teeth. "You sent them to the sheriff, right?"

"I wanted to answer it." She paused a second. "I wanted to hear what she had to say."

That, he'd known. "Would it have been honest, or would she just be stringing you along still? Pretending to be your friend while she helps hold this town hostage."

She screamed, "I wanted to talk to her!"

"I know." Drew kept his voice even. He found the turn off, a blind corner. No brakes, not until the last second. He pressed them hard and swung the wheel to the right in one movement. Then he hit the gas. The tires spun out for a second but caught in the gravel of the parking lot. Drew shut his headlights off, not needing them to see where he was going considering he'd been driving this route since he got his license.

He made his way to a space far to the right, out of sight, and shoved the car in park. He flashed the headlights once. A teen boy swung off a horse. He held the reins to another horse and stood beside it.

Craig let the reins go and turned his own horse before he walked the animal away. Out of sight. The neighbor kid took a ridiculously low amount of money for all the ways he helped Drew out, taking care of the animal when he couldn't. They'd met out on the trail, Craig's parent's ranch not a half a mile from here—so Drew didn't worry about the young man getting home. He had a good dad, but Drew still saw that seed of something wild in him. The same thing he saw in the mirror.

He'd picked his trainee. Drew and Craig were going to start working some local investigations together this summer, when the kid had finished out his junior year.

"Let's go."

She cracked the car door. He came around and took her hand before he walked her to the horse. "Hey, Spring." He laid a hand on the side of her neck. The horse moved her head close to his, taking in his scent. "Your breath smells like apples."

He climbed on, then held a hand out for Ellie.

"Where are we going?" She sounded sad. And lost.

"Somewhere safe."

She put her foot in the stirrup, and he braced her weight while she swung on. There was a second of hesitation, then her arms slid around his.

A truck pulled into the parking lot.

Drew kicked with his heels, and Spring set off. He urged her faster, but not too fast. It was dangerous for her to go that speed with the lack of light. They knew this trail, though. Just like Craig knew the way home.

He felt Ellie's hands slacken. He grabbed them and patted her hand. "Talk to me. Don't fall asleep." She would end up falling off.

"I told her everything. I—" Her voice broke. "I trusted her. Cried with her."

"I know."

Her arms tightened.

Drew said, "Tell me."

"I had this boyfriend in college." Her voice was soft, but broken. "I got pregnant. He seemed happy, and we went to the courthouse. Got married."

Drew's stomach clenched. She was married?

"A few weeks later, I—" Her voice broke.

Drew waited, aware she was drumming up the courage to trust him with something as painful as her best friend's betrayal. Maybe even more so.

"I lost the baby."

Drew tightened his grip on her hand and tugged her body closer to his. She needed the comfort, as well as the warmth.

"He filed for divorce. After all," she choked the words out. "What reason was there to stay?"

"I'm sorry." He was. Drew was *so* sorry. Though, maybe it should have been Laney who was apologizing. He was still right to have tossed that phone out the window. Who knew how far their reach extended? She said nothing for awhile, then her quiet voice finally asked, "Where are we going?"

"My place, to restock supplies. Weapons and ammo." And they were almost there. "Then we're on the road again. Staying in one place is dangerous."

"Okay." Her voice sounded hollow. Empty in a way that threatened to break his heart.

"Then we'll finish this, yeah?"

He felt her nod against the back of his jacket. Both of them were so far past worn out it was a wonder they were still functioning. His hip smarted from the motion of the horse. When he got off, his leg would likely collapse. Ellie had a huge bruise—he would bet—from the gunshot. And that knife wound.

Mark was on his way. Alvarez was already here with Ellie's dad.

The four of them, plus Will and the current sheriff, could do this. *We can do this, right Lord?* Despite what he'd said to Ellie, Drew had doubts.

Especially by the time they got to his cabin.

"Your house is on fire."

16

The air hung thick with the smell of smoke. Ellie's eyes stung. She blinked away the gathering tears. "I'm sorry."

Drew tugged on the reins, and they continued on before anyone saw them. Around the area in front of his house, he headed toward the road. He pulled out his phone and made a call. But not without a glance at her, full of feeling. She nodded. He asked the state police dispatcher for emergency services then hung up abruptly.

"So my phone goes out the window, but you're allowed to keep yours?" The comment slipped out. Would she even have wanted to hold it back? Ellie wasn't sure. Drew seemed to have some interesting ideas as to how all this was going to go down. And not much of it adhered to the rules she was bound to as a sheriff's deputy.

"It's unregistered. So I can communicate with Mark under the radar."

A burner phone? Of course it was. She rolled her eyes, because he couldn't see her behind him.

Probably she could be a little more sympathetic about the fact all his worldly belongings were going up in flames. Ellie just couldn't bring herself to feel that loss as well—even in sympathy. Far too much had gone on tonight. She was primarily reacting to the fact she'd laid her soul bare to him. Now Ellie had hit the point where her brain wanted to shut down. Where her heart felt the need to just be numb and avoid feeling anything at all—at least until she could process it.

Drew knew about the baby she had lost. It was years ago now, more than six.

Her heart squeezed, but inside she just felt…cold. She'd grieved long and hard. Moved on with her life. And then in one moment, it all came rushing back. The child inside her. The loss. The betrayal. Maybe it would touch her like this every so often for the rest of her life. A reminder of the disaster. All the ways she had failed, things she hadn't forgiven herself for. Things she hadn't received God's offer of forgiveness for, preferring to stay where she could feel the pain. So that she could remember.

But that wasn't honoring the life she'd had inside her.

Drew walked the horse to the driveway and headed toward the road. Ellie pulled her arms from around his waist and adjusted her weight. Antsy for something…maybe a fight. That would certainly release some tension, though getting physical would end quickly given the state she was in. And it wasn't like she was going to fight Drew.

Maybe he would let her use the phone. "Can I call my dad with that?"

"In a minute. Let's figure out where we're going to go next."

She bit her lips together for a second. "We could double back to the truck."

"That's probably going to be our best shot at staying mobile if they're rallying. They could be spread all over town, looking for us."

"So they know who we are, and now they're trying to kill us. That it?"

He shrugged one shoulder, the one in front of her face. "Getting back at us." He paused. "Not many other reasons they'd need to burn down Eric and Alma's house."

"It's *your* house."

"I rent it from them."

"So that means you don't care about it? Or any of your stuff?"

He sighed. "I'm not the one out money."

"No, just all your personal possessions." How was that not being out money? He'd have to pay to replace them, wouldn't he?

She'd been inside his house. There wasn't much beyond furniture that she'd seen. Some artwork on the walls—photos he had printed for himself. Then a thought occurred to her. She gasped. "Your camera."

"Okay *that* I care about. There were a couple of pictures on there I hadn't uploaded yet. It was on my dining table."

They were back on the trail now, and it wasn't long before they reached the truck. At least, they could see it.

He pulled the horse to a stop before they'd even emerged from the trees. "Hop off."

Ellie slid to the ground and locked her knees to keep from crumpling.

"Hopefully the fire department can put the fire out quickly. I wouldn't want it to spread and cause problems."

There was no wind, and it was cold tonight. The risk of wildfire was low. Plus, he probably had safeguards around his house to keep low hanging trees close by from being reached by embers. Nothing was perfect but measures could be taken. And knowing Drew, he probably kept up with that stuff.

"Do you see anyone?"

Ellie drew her weapon. The last thing she wanted was to be caught unawares. She scanned the area. No other vehicles. No flashlight beams. She couldn't hear talking or even the crack of branches that might indicate someone walking around.

She shook her head. "Nothing."

He took the saddle off his horse and removed all the tack. Then he rubbed all the way down both her sides. He stepped back and yelled, "Yah!" With a loud slap on her rump. The horse darted forward, to the trail. In a couple of steps she slowed, then looked back.

Drew threw the saddle over his shoulder with a grunt and headed for his truck. Ellie picked up what was left and followed him. "You're just going to leave her out here?"

"Spring knows the way home, though she might not want to stick around with the smoke smell. She can keep herself safe until I can find her. Or until Craig does."

"That's it?"

He hauled the saddle into the bed of his truck. "What do you want me to say? I don't particularly want to leave her out here, but I have no choice."

"You're abandoning her."

"Do you have a horse trailer in your pocket? Because I don't."

"You could call that neighbor kid."

"It's the middle of the night, Ellie. I'm not waking Craig up."

"He wouldn't understand because your house is on fire?"

"Why are we arguing about this?" He waved to the door. "Get in the truck. We're exposed standing out here."

She set her hands on her hips. "I'm the one with a badge."

He walked toward her, not stopping. His momentum forced her back to the passenger door. "Get in." Teeth flashed in the moonlight, and he pulled the door open.

Ellie got in. Drew rounded the front of the truck and got in the driver's side. He pushed out a breath, turning the key in the ignition. "The person you're mad at is Laney. Not me."

The radio came on.

"…for the following counties."

"Emergency alert." Ellie turned it down so it wasn't as loud.

The electronic voice listed a number of counties, then said, "All residents are instructed to remain in their homes until further notice. Do not approach any unknown persons. The fugitive at large is armed and extremely dangerous. Law enforcement personnel are attempting to apprehend him. Please remain in your homes."

The message repeated from there. A hastily assembled emergency alert designed to clear the streets of anyone who shouldn't be there. Which was why the highway was practically empty.

"They're looking for us."

"I think they're probably looking for me." Drew's voice was strained when he added, "They're going to find us."

But he didn't sound scared. He sounded determined.

"You want them to."

"It's the only way to end this. They know I'm not going to join up with them now."

Ellie stared at the outline of his features in the dark cab of the truck. Strong jaw, set with that determination she'd heard in his voice. Doubt crept in, but Ellie wanted to believe he'd come into her life again now for a reason. For God to do something she hadn't allowed Him to do before. "So what's the plan?"

————

As MUCH AS he pretended otherwise, he didn't like leaving his horse. Ellie didn't need to add to that emotion though. Too much stress would split their focus. Right now he needed to put aside the concern as to what would happen to Spring and fix the problem he could handle.

Afterward, he'd go out and find her.

Then he'd have to figure out what he was going to do about his burned-out house. Eric and Alma would tell him that the important thing was he wasn't hurt. The rent money he paid them was next to nothing. They probably wouldn't want to rebuild, considering they'd never made money on the house. And wouldn't, if he kept living there.

They could pocket the insurance money instead. Sell off the land—but not to these people who'd put an emergency alert out on the airwaves. All to try and lessen the number of residents outside tonight. Did they want a showdown? Drew was going to give them one.

He appreciated that they didn't want the uninvolved caught in the crossfire, but he didn't think that was it. He figured they probably just wanted it to be easier to find him and Ellie. Everyone out on the streets tonight was either one of them or the enemy.

Drew stopped at the light to turn onto Main Street. "The sheriff's office. We still need supplies." Protective vests. Ammo. Contact with the state police might help but could they run the risk of these people not having the state police in their pocket? Calling about a fire was one thing. This was entirely different.

Mark was on his way. That help was what Drew was

counting on. He needed to round up Mark—and Alvarez, who was protecting Ellie's father. Then they could get the help of the former sheriff, if he was able, and Sheriff Burgess.

That had to be enough because it was all they had.

He eased off the brake and they rolled through the intersection. But Drew didn't turn down Main Street. Instead, he headed for the street behind the sheriff's office. If anyone was on or around the grassy area in the middle of Main, keeping watch for them, then they needed to steer clear of it. Take the back entrance. Raid the sheriff's department for what they needed.

Assuming someone else hadn't done that before them.

He parked and they sat for a second, both looking around. "It's weird not seeing anyone."

Ellie nodded. "So weird. The place is completely deserted."

The parking lot where sheriff's department vehicles were parked contained only one right now. The boss's SUV was here. "Does that mean the sheriff is inside?"

Ellie said, "Maybe. But not definitely."

"I guess we'll find out." He grabbed the door handle. "I want to find out."

Movement caught his attention. He climbed out and spotted a shadowy figure dart out of an alley beside the sheriff's office. Drew's leg throbbed as he headed for the shadows up against the building. He saw the figure pull out a phone and put it to his ear. "It's done."

The figure hung up, then started to run faster away from the sheriff's office. What was done?

Drew changed direction. It grated on him to let the guy get away, but he had to know what had been "done" inside. Ellie was out of the car. "What is it?"

He didn't like this. Didn't even want to voice his fears aloud. "We need to get in there."

They quickly made their way to the back door. It was locked. Drew lifted his foot and kicked the door open. Ellie made her way up the stairs first.

The main office was dark. She crept in, gun drawn. Neither of them had more than a couple of bullets left. It had been a really long day.

She glanced back, then made some hand motions. Drew nodded. She headed left. He checked to the right. "Clear."

"In here."

He met her at the door. Her body had gone stiff. Then she seemed to snap out of it.

The lamp on the sheriff's desk was on. He was tied to his chair, and it was obvious he'd suffered before they shot him in the stomach. Drew sighed. A long and painful death wasn't how he'd choose to put someone out of their misery, but he supposed that made sense for these people.

And Laney was tied up in this? He would guess she had a good explanation, but whether Ellie would want to hear it was another question.

The sheriff's body shifted. His lips parted and his chest rattled with the intake of breath.

Ellie hesitated, her fingers stretched out, ready to take his pulse. "He's alive." She touched the sheriff's shoulders. "Hank, can you hear me?"

No answer came, just that rattling inhale. Not good.

Drew said, "I'm going to raid the gun cage." Either way they would need supplies.

She nodded but didn't turn back from the sheriff. She heard him run to the door on the far side of the sheriff's office. When he returned, it was with arms full of weapons. Ammo in every pocket. Two vests slung over one shoulder.

Ellie had a towel pressed against the sheriff's stomach. His desk phone was between her ear and shoulder.

"Yes. Everyone." She paused. "I don't care. Things are out of control here. We're getting ready to go to war, and we need backup." She hung up the phone and glanced at him. "Whether they're going to send anyone, I don't know. And I can't waste the time trying to decipher whether or not they've been compromised."

"You're right." He handed her a vest. "Not when the mayor or someone else could have called them, or any of these other people we know now are involved." He looked at the sheriff. "Can they get an ambulance in? Can we?"

"The state police Lieutenant said he'll alert Life Flight. They'll send a chopper in to get the sheriff." She paused. "I don't like leaving him."

"Me either."

"He's barely hanging on," she said, tears in her voice. "What they did to him…" Her words trailed off and her voice hitched.

"Ellie."

The name came from the sheriff's lips.

"Sheriff." She turned to him. "Help is on the way."

He tried to shake his head.

"No. Stay still. The state police are sending Life Flight." She spoke as though she were attempting to reassure herself. "I hope."

"I'm praying." Drew squeezed her shoulder then looked over the sheriff. He knew next to nothing about how to stabilize someone. Why hadn't he taken that medical training course the feds had offered to send him on? It certainly could have come in handy right now.

"Ellie."

"Don't try to speak," she told him.

He took another inhale, then coughed, his body wracked with spasms.

"Who did this to you?"

"Call…"

Drew said, "Where's your phone?"

"Took…it."

"Who do you need to call?"

"Will." The sheriff said, "Warn…him."

"Ellie's father is a target?" Drew asked. The man had a US Marshal with him, and Alvarez wasn't about to allow either of them to get hurt. Drew was more worried about him and Ellie right now.

The sheriff said, "All. Are."

"Okay. Don't worry." Drew said it even though they should all be very worried. "We're going to finish this."

"Safe."

Ellie said, "We're not done until the town is safe. You stay with us, we're getting help."

His eyes shut, as though the last of his strength was gone now. Overhead the low drone of a helicopter could be heard. Drew looked out the window. "Life Flight."

He wanted to ask the sheriff if he'd been pressured by the group into ruling Natalie Benson's death a suicide. But there would be time for that later.

Once they had the EMTs in, taking care of the sheriff and getting him ready to transport, Drew snagged Ellie's elbow. "We've gotta go."

She nodded, not taking her eyes from her boss. "If they have his phone, then they have the photos that I sent him. The ones that were on mine that you threw out the window. All of our evidence."

They didn't have time for a debate or an argument. "You have online backup, right?"

"My storage is full. Nothing is uploading right now."

He sighed. "We have to go."

The EMTs carried the sheriff out the door, upstairs to the roof where the chopper had landed. Drew handed over his phone to her. "Call your dad."

She did. He heard it ring against her ear.

"No answer?"

She nodded.

"That's what I was afraid of."

17

E llie banged on the glass of the hospital's main entrance. "Let us in."

The security guard shook his head. "Can't, Miss. I'm sorry. Dangerous fugitive on the loose, and we're on lockdown."

She pulled the badge from her back pocket. She slammed it so hard it cracked against the glass. "Let us in."

His gaze shifted to the gold star badge. "How do I know he ain't the fugitive, and you're letting him in because he's forcing you?" He motioned to Drew, over her shoulder.

"I'm not under duress." She took a breath even though she wanted to scream. "Let. Us. In."

He took a step back and scratched at his jaw. "I dunno —"

Ellie pulled her weapon and pointed it at the glass of the door but aimed at the carpet inside. "Back up. I'm going to shoot the glass out."

"Okay. Okay." He moved to the door handle, but not before she lowered her weapon. Then he reached for it, and let them in.

Ellie barreled past him. She wasn't going to explain, and she wasn't going to justify herself. She was going to do her job. This security guy would have to like it or not.

"Wanna show me some ID?"

She looked back to see he'd asked this of Drew.

Her partner shook his head. "No." Then moved past the security guard to stand at her side.

Ellie turned back to the wide-eyed lady at the front desk. Her face was the same salmon color as her floral sweater. She looked like a Sunday school teacher.

"Sorry about all that." Ellie flashed her badge again and tried not to look as stressed out as she was. "I need some help. Can you look someone up on that thing?" She motioned to the computer.

"Sure, but if you're asking about your father, Deputy Maxwell, there's…" She swallowed. "Well, there's something the nice security guard needs to tell you."

"I woulda gotten there." He rocked back on his heels. "If you'd let me."

She turned back to the lady. "Maybe you could tell me."

Now. Or Ellie's head was liable to explode.

"He was checked out of the hospital. Though, not exactly checked out. They didn't fill out any paperwork. The doctors tried to stop the men, and—"

"Someone kidnapped my father?"

"Well…" Her gaze darted about, then came back to meet Ellie's. "That is… Yes."

Drew said, "And the man who was with him. Plain clothes. He's a federal marshal."

"Oh." Her eyebrows drew together. "There was a man left in the room. Could that be him?"

"Probably."

She sent a polite smile in Drew's direction. "He sustained

a pretty significant head injury. He's being assessed right now."

Drew pulled out his phone and stepped away.

The receptionist shifted to face Ellie. "We called the state police. They said they'd send someone over, but its been half an hour."

"So he was taken out of here before the lockdown order came in?"

Sunday school teacher lady nodded. "Its part of the reason we didn't question it. Something's going on in town, and we have all these people to keep safe. But then we found that other man still in the room."

"You'd have questioned it normally?"

"The hospital's doors should always be open." She lifted her chin. Ellie wondered what had happened in her life to make her spine shore up like that. A judgment about the world she lived in, born out of the adversity she had lived.

Ellie said, "Keep the front door and the emergency bay open. Life Flight should be bringing in the sheriff."

"He was rerouted out of town. They said he was stable enough they could take the extra couple of minutes for the journey."

And if he hadn't been? Ellie didn't want to know what would have happened if the sheriff didn't make it. She could hardly do this by herself.

She had Drew. For now, that would be enough.

Ellie took a step back, away from the desk and the three people who stood around it. She needed a moment to clear her head.

Could they talk to the injured man and see what he could tell them? Maybe he was too hurt. She prayed he wasn't permanently damaged by a battle that had nothing to do with him. And if they could get the IDs of the people who had taken her father, would that help find him?

She needed contact. Like a ransom call.

Ellie motioned to Drew with her fingers. He was done with his call now. She said, "I need your phone."

He studied her with a questioning gaze, but said nothing as he handed it over.

She dialed Laney's cell phone number from memory. Her friend had gotten the phone number long ago. Back when phone numbers still needed to be memorized, a fact Ellie thanked God for now. She'd called her friend regularly from their landline at home back in those days.

She dialed it now, knowing this conversation would be nothing like their past conversations. Everything about their relationship had changed. Laney was part of a group destroying this town. A group who had forced Brad and Sheila from their homes…and how many others?

They were responsible for the receptionist's death.

Laney had stood there, along with Deputy Coughlan. Neither of them had done anything while Alan Franz shot Simon Mills in cold blood.

No, Simon may not have been a good person. But no one deserved to be murdered. That's why the law didn't have clarifications for a victim's moral character. No one had the right to take a life unless it was to protect themselves or someone else. The way Drew had protected her, shooting the gunman dressed as a security guard. Maybe he'd been a real security guard, she didn't know.

A man answered the phone. "Deputy Maxwell."

"Who is this?"

"If you want your father back, you'll come to the bowling alley."

"That's it?" she said. "I show up, and you give him back to me?"

Drew shifted closer. His body was warm. Even though

they weren't touching, it was a comfort to her. She wanted to sink into his embrace, but things were insane. If she didn't have focus, she wasn't going to be able to do this.

They had no help, unless Mark showed up fast or the state police sent an army. And the clock was ticking. Who knew what they were doing—or planning to do—with her father?

"If you don't show up, I guess you'll never find out. Will you?"

She gritted her teeth together. "You'll probably just kill him, and then us too?"

Drew set his hand on her shoulder. Behind her other shoulder, the security guard got close. An entirely different sensation than Drew being there. She shifted away from him, closer to Drew. His hand slipped across the back of her shoulders, and she collided with his side. He held her there.

"I want to speak with him." She *had* to know he was at least still alive.

"He's unavailable right now."

"Then too bad. You get nothing." She balled her free hand into fists, nursing the anger. "You should have left him in the hospital. Now you'll have another death on your hands."

"Is that right?"

She took a breath. "I want to speak to Laney. Now."

He chuckled. She thought she recognized the voice but couldn't be sure. "Guess you don't know what *we* want."

"I'm not playing your game."

"Then you best show up."

The line went dead.

———

DREW HIT SEND on the text so Mark would know where they were headed. In a couple of seconds, he got a reply.

TWENTY-FIVE MINUTES.

He relayed that to Ellie as they crossed the street, headed for the bowling alley. She shook her head. "That's a long time."

He agreed. "Too long to wait."

They halted at the side door, and he eyed the surveillance camera in the loading area. Were they watching? Either they already knew he and Ellie were there, or they would soon enough.

He pushed the door open, and she went in first. He had no problem playing a protective role here. Ellie had the weight of her badge behind her actions, even with what these people had tried to do. What they'd *been* doing for years. Subverting the law for their own financial gains.

They moved into the main hall inside of the bowling alley. Most of the lights were out, except for runners down the sides of the lanes.

"Dad!"

Drew spotted what she had seen. What she now raced toward. Her father was slumped on the floor in the center of the room. She knelt beside him. "He's alive." Her voice carried back to Drew.

"Good." He didn't go to her, though.

Out the corner of his eye he saw movement. By the time he glanced over, the movement was gone. He checked all corners. Hiding spots. In the darkness there could be any number of people in here.

Drew held his gun loose in his hand. Providing cover fire would be his role here. Though the last thing he wanted was to get into a gunfight with Ellie exposed like that.

He called out, "Can you move him?"

"No. We need help."

They could carry him out together. But something about this didn't sit right with him. Drew took half a dozen steps. Put himself out in the open. Then he called out to whoever was waiting. Hiding. "Come out, now."

No one moved.

"Lay down your weapons and come out where we can see you. This is over. Let's not make things worse before it's over."

He took another step.

The lights flickered on. Multicolored strobes flashed in a rhythm, the ones used on cosmic bowling night. Ellie dipped into shadow, and then reappeared, though she hadn't moved at all.

The strobes spun and swirled, destroying any chance he had of spotting anyone.

Still, there was nothing making noise much above silence.

He called out again. "Let's end this before—"

Music came on. It was like being in a concert when even that was turned up too loud. He winced. Ducked back into the shadows. Wherever they were, he'd have to root them out.

He wanted to call to Ellie to stay put, but figured she would likely remain with her father. He hoped.

God, help me.

He skirted the edge of the room to look for anyone hiding and made his way around the perimeter. Take out the stragglers first. Work his way to whoever was calling the shots.

The first man rose up in front of him. Drew grabbed the guy. He dipped his head, rotated his shoulders and flipped the man over him and onto his back on the floor. Out cold. He pulled zip ties from his pocket, ignored the ones that spilled onto the ground, and tied the man's hands behind his back.

The next one never even saw him coming.

Drew wrapped an arm around his neck from behind and put the man in a sleeper hold. It wasn't long before his body slumped, and Drew laid him on the ground. Secured his hands.

The third got in a punch. Drew hit him on the temple with his weapon, breathing hard. Sweat rolled down his back under the vest and dampened his T-shirt.

He sucked in a few full breaths and continued on. How many were there? Enough for an ambush, and yet they'd waited out of sight. For what?

Drew neared the office. Was the person in charge inside? Calling the shots one step removed wasn't the way Drew worked—which was why he had no employees. When he did get Craig as a protégé, things were going to be different than the way his Uncle Merrick had done things. Some of his crazy ideas about what made a man strong were just insane.

He prayed for Ellie and her father. For the chance to show Craig what his life was like. To find another person who would fully understand Drew Turner-North, and who he really was.

He wanted that chance.

And the chance to tell Ellie how he truly felt.

Whether she felt the same or not, he didn't know. But he wanted her to know how he felt. After all, she knew him now in a way not many people did. Maybe that would grow to more. *God, that's what I want.* If it was His will, Drew would have what he needed to get them through this.

The alternative didn't bear thinking about.

A man came out of nowhere. The arm that swung at him came from the dark too late for him to weave his head to the side. White light flashed across his vision. His leg buckled. He bent the knee of his other leg and then pushed off the ground.

He launched his body at the man, and they hit the thin

carpet on the floor. Momentum carried them over and over. Pain exploded in his hip. His knee. He cried out but got a grip on the man. Enough to twist the guy's arm back far enough that he was the one to cry out this time.

Drew leaned on the man's back, careful not to put weight on his knee.

The music cut out, as did the flashing lights. Then regular fluorescents switched on.

"Drew!" Ellie's voice rang out, high and full of fear.

He finished securing the man he'd brought down and then stood. She was in the center with her father where he'd left her. Alan Franz held her arm, his gun pointed at her chin.

Fear rushed through him. It was like having an ice bucket dumped over his head. Or the time a semi had drifted across the center lane, right at him. The split second realization that everything in his world was about to change.

God had saved him from that semi. And so many other things that should have killed him. Or could have killed him. Would he do that now, or had Drew's time run out? Was he going to watch Ellie die, an end to God's goodness in his life?

Drew stepped over the man on the floor and out toward the bowling lanes. "Okay." He held his hands up.

Ellie craned her neck back. Franz had it in his grip. Her holster was empty, her gun discarded too far for her to reach.

Franz said, "Drop that gun."

Drew didn't want to, but what was the alternative? He bent and laid it down, wincing at the feel of his hip and knee. "Okay, it's down. Now let her go."

The man who'd shot Simon Mills grinned. His suit was rumpled. Hair askew. A murderer who had lived in their town this whole time. Hiding behind the scenes, doing whatever he wanted. Believing he would never get caught.

"It's over," Drew said. "Let her go."

There was a rush of movement behind him. Ellie's eyes widened. Drew didn't have time to turn. Something hard slammed into the back of his head.

Black swallowed him up, and he felt his own body hit the ground.

18

E verything in her screamed. It took a second, then the sound emerged from her mouth. As though her body had to catch up with what her mind was experiencing.

The man who'd come up behind Drew and struck him stood over his body. Her partner was out cold. She could see the glistening wet on the back of his head. Blood.

Franz gripped her elbow. "Shut up."

She forced herself to quit screaming. On the floor close by, her father moaned. Her gun. She couldn't reach any of them.

Franz dragged her back. Farther away from what she needed. *Who* she needed. Her dad. Drew. More tears rolled down her face as she struggled against Franz's grip. He hauled her along. She kicked at his leg with her boot heel. Would the other guy shoot her? Franz winced but kept going, shoving the gun against her ribs. "I'll shoot you."

Then why didn't the bank-manager-turned-murderer just do it? "What do you want?"

"Just keep moving."

"I don't have land," she said. "I'm not going to sell you anything."

He glanced back, the gun still pressed painfully against her side. "Bring him."

She tried to twist back. Pain lanced through her side. She gritted her teeth and managed to look behind her, far enough to see the man who had hit Drew haul her father onto his shoulder. He followed them, leaving Drew on the floor.

They were bringing her father?

They were leaving Drew and bringing her father.

Franz called out again. "Kill that one!"

Her foot clipped a stair and she fell, landing on her side on the steps up to the food court area. Franz pulled on her arm. "Get up!"

Could she stall long enough for help to come? Mark was on his way, right? Or maybe Drew could rally and fight back against them. He wasn't dead. He *couldn't* be. She had a gun pressed to her ribs. If she did anything other than what the bank manager told her to, he would not miss.

Ellie planted her hands and got her feet under her. She tried to breathe, tried to figure out how this was going to go and what she was supposed to do.

There was nothing in her training about being kidnapped at gunpoint by someone you'd gone to about maybe getting a mortgage. Franz was supposed to be an upstanding member of the community.

A gunshot rang out. She turned and saw a pistol in the hand of a man who stood over Drew's body. "No!"

He shoved her toward the door.

She stumbled again.

He pushed her on, toward a van. She hit the passenger door and turned. "Did you force them all to be part of your group?"

"Get in."

"You killed Simon Mills, and now Drew is dead, too. What else have you done? The receptionist, maybe? Did you kill Natalie Barnes?" It was all she could do to keep her thoughts in line, to keep her voice from completely breaking. The way her heart had just done.

She had to challenge him. Let him know she wasn't going to go down without a fight—one that would end with him in handcuffs.

"I thought that was ruled a suicide."

She said, "Rulings can change."

Obviously the sheriff had been pressured into making that call. Who knew what the evidence indicated? She was going to look into that personally.

If she got out of this alive.

A shadow landed on the sidewalk as Laney slid the door open. Her friend's features were dark tonight, as dark as the night sky.

Nausea rolled through Ellie's stomach. "How could you—"

Franz shoved her.

Ellie's shins slammed against the edge of the van and she fell in, crying out. Pain ricocheted through her. All those bruises. Cuts. Injuries. More tears gathered, but she wouldn't let them fall. She was done being weak. Drew was dead, and after all this time, she was done hiding her pain beneath a façade that wasn't real.

Ellie roared in frustration. "Why are you doing this?"

Franz stood at the open van door, gun pointed at her. "Scoot in." He shifted the hand holding his gun to point it at Laney. "Or you both die."

Laney sucked in a breath.

Ellie scrambled farther into the van. The other man dumped her father beside her. Franz slid the door shut and got in the passenger seat. "Drive!"

They swayed as the van driver—Deputy Coughlan—hit the gas. Laney's body leaned against her, the pressure of her friend's weight adding to her injuries.

"Get off me."

"Sorry." She shifted, enough to quit leaning on Ellie. "I'm sorry."

Ellie moved to stroke her father's cheek. "You should have thought about that before you joined up with these people." She gritted her teeth, pushed off the floor of the van and sat up to lean against the side. "These *murderers*."

"I didn't want this, Ellie. You have to know that."

She ignored the tears in her friend's voice. "Do you know how many criminals say that to me? But only *after* they've destroyed people's lives."

"I know what I've done." Laney looked away.

"Why?" she asked. "For what?"

"Money of course. How do you think my business stays afloat? My dad was part of the group. I inherited the position after he died." She sucked in a breath and kept whispering. "It's not all bad. When they're done with a mining project they make the area a wilderness sanctuary. They donate money to schools and scholarships."

"And their own pockets."

"Without it, I'd be bankrupt. I would have had to close my doors."

Like that was a reason to join up with people like Alan Franz, whose end game was hurting others. Not that they hadn't been actively doing so all along. Sure, people who'd sold their lands had been compensated, like Brad and Sheila currently in Acapulco. But what had that compensation cost them? Sheila hadn't wanted to move. She'd been forced out.

Some residents had no doubt lived on land that'd been in their family for generations. Who thought about that cost when they wanted mining and then a wildlife sanctuary? As though doing that made it all okay.

At the end of the day, Laney and her friends were lining their own pockets. They weren't out to benefit anyone else.

"I thought you were a good person." Ellie stared at her friend, desperate to see something beyond the words she thought Ellie wanted to hear. "I trusted you."

Tears spilled down Laney's cheeks. "El…" her voice broke in the middle of Ellie's name.

Her heart squeezed. But it was too late for Laney to feel bad. She was too deep in this to get the privilege of feeling guilty. That wasn't going to change all that she was responsible for. And maybe Ellie was just jaded, dealing with criminals more than she did regular folks on most days. So many of them talked a good game. They just said what you wanted to hear.

Maybe Laney was having this change of heart because Alan Franz had threatened to kill her, as well as Ellie. Or because she was finally seeing that things had gone too far. Maybe her remorse was genuine.

But Ellie couldn't accept it. Not right now, not when her father was lying beside her unconscious. When Drew was back at the bowling alley, dead from that gunshot.

There was no room in her heart to work through this. She needed help.

God, Drew needs Your help. Even if he was already dead, she could still pray, still hope.

So do I.

Wherever they were going, and whatever was going to happen when they got there, Ellie knew it wasn't going to be good.

She leaned over and touched her father's shoulder.

Would any of them survive this?

———

PAIN. So much pain. Was this what Ellie had felt when she was shot? Point blank range, closer than she'd been hit.

Consciousness swam in front of him, his brain attempting to fire when it also wanted to shut down completely. The man stood over him and had laughed.

Shot him, and then laughed.

Some joke.

"This is gonna be fun."

Then he'd dragged Drew into the office and left. *What on earth?* Drew patted his pockets, grateful his thoughts had finally settled down. It was like trying to think through the fog of a concussion.

Ellie was gone.

He'd heard her scream. She thought he was dead, but he was alive and determined to find her. There was no way he'd leave her to Alan Franz. Alan would destroy her life the way he'd done to so many others.

No phone. They had to have taken it. No knife. No other weapons. Where was Mark? Shouldn't he have shown up already?

Drew heard movement in the hall outside the office. Time to move. He grabbed the edge of the desk, planted the foot of his good leg and hoisted himself to stand. Though, not without the little hop required to get his balance. Now he just needed a weapon.

He moved to the door. When the man entered, Drew grabbed the door and whipped it forward. The wood smacked the man in the forehead.

Drew hit him again, then grabbed his wrist—the one holding the gun. The same gun he'd fired at Drew's chest just for fun. The man slammed back against the door from his side. It glanced off Drew's shoulder, but he ignored it and wrestled for control of the gun.

Everything blurred into a wash of sensations. The smell of sweat. Movements became instinctual, as life and death hung on the edge of a knife. Fights were about so much instinct they were often over before Drew even really contemplated the fact they'd started.

He balled his fist and slammed it into the man's stomach in an uppercut. His feet left the ground, but he kicked back.

One boot hit Drew's swollen knee.

He cried out.

The other man jumped on this, an admission of weakness that could be exploited. And a man who shot someone at point blank range just for fun was all about exploiting a weakness.

Drew's knee threatened to buckle. He hit the man again, but the guy was already moving. He used his free hand to punch Drew in the temple, then stomped again with his boot.

Drew cried out. His legs buckled. He planted one hand on the office carpet, pushed off his good foot and barreled into the guy.

The man's back hit the wall.

The gun went off.

Two other men rushed into the room. Guys he'd tied up earlier. Drew didn't quit fighting this one. Not until the others had his arms pinned back. They dragged him to the far wall and held him there.

The man he'd been fighting stood straight. Brushed off the front of his shirt. His upper lip curled, but he wasted no time lifting his gun.

It went off, the boom echoing through the room. Drew waited for the pain as the bullet hit him.

But it never came.

He opened his eyes and saw the surprise on the man's face. A red stain began its slow spread across his chest.

He fell to the ground.

The other two let go of his arms and launched forward. A man stepped into the room. He shot one, then the other.

Drew nearly collapsed, but the floor was kind of crowded. "Mark?"

His friend's lips pressed into a line. "I think this clears off all debts. Everything I owe you."

"Except the pizza."

Mark shook his head. "No mushrooms this time." He held out his hand. Drew took it, partly a shake and partly his needing a steady hand to aid his movement across the room. "Not sure I've ever seen you look worse than this."

Drew grabbed a chair and sat. He held up a hand and for a few moments just breathed. Adrenaline subsided, leaving shakiness in its wake. An awareness of all the new places he'd just gained bruises. It felt like his whole body was one big injury.

Sweat rolled down his temple. He swiped it away with a gritty hand. "Ellie." She probably thought he was dead. They'd taken her. But where?

"That your girl, the deputy?"

"Yeah." She was his girl. He wanted to find her so he could tell her how he felt. No more of this back and forth. She needed to know that he was more than halfway in love with her right now.

Especially with her, "No" still ringing in his ears. She thought he was dead. He'd heard heartbreak and the wealth of her feelings for him in that one word. It hurt to think she was in pain right now, thinking he was dead.

I need to set her straight, Lord. Find her and make her safe. After that…well, he wouldn't mind the chance to kiss her. And to see how she felt about him. Hear her say it out loud, not just listen to the look in her eyes every time she turned that gaze his way.

"So you wanna go find her," Mark said, "or are you going to sit in that chair all night?"

"I don't know where they took her."

"I'm sure there's a live one. I didn't kill them all." He headed for the hallway, his FBI suit shifting as he moved. Mark had always spent far too much on clothes but he claimed the more expensive they were, the better they felt. Drew preferred his jeans and the shirt he'd bought at the grocery superstore two towns over.

That only made him wonder what Ellie's stance was on all that. She was hardly a heels and purse kind of woman, but what did he know? Drew wanted the chance to find out. Take her to that steak place and get the chance for them both to dress up.

Mark tapped his fingers on the side of his leg. "Seriously. Come *on*."

Drew got up, swayed. Sat back down.

"Yeah. Scratch that. Stay there, I'll be back."

True to his word, his federal agent friend reappeared a minute or two later and shoved a guy to the floor in front of Drew. "Talk."

The man spat. In whose direction it was supposed to have gone, Drew wasn't sure.

"Where did they take Deputy Maxwell?"

"How should I know?" The man's handlebar mustache twitched even when he wasn't speaking.

"You *know*." Drew motioned to Mark. "And this special agent with the FBI is going to prove it."

"I got two strikes." He glanced between them. "I can't go down again."

"Guess you should've thought about that before you took a job working for a bunch of people *breaking the law*. People who want you to do their dirty work." Drew let his frustration bleed into the words. "And unless you want to be charged with accessory to the murder of a sheriff's deputy on top of everything else, then you'd better start talking."

The mustache moved again.

"Maybe we should just kill him, find another one," Mark suggested.

Drew had seen that look in his eyes. He wasn't serious. But the guy on the floor didn't know that. "So what's it gonna be?" He motioned to the guys Mark had shot. "End up like them. Go to prison for the rest of your life…or tell me where they took her."

He glanced at Mark. Or, more specifically, at Mark's weapon that was pointed at him. Then he looked at Drew. "Fine. I'll tell you what I know."

19

Ellie crawled across the carpet to her father. They were in a house. A brand new house that seemed to be still under construction. Near as she could tell this was a complex of townhouses, maybe the one on the outskirts of town. Upmarket residences no one who worked in town would be able to afford. So who would buy them?

She didn't care what Alan's business plan involved. Not right now, anyway. Later on she would use the law to come up against this. No matter what the outdoorsy-types who worked remotely, and their disposable incomes, did for the local economy.

"Dad." She patted his cheek, scared to wake him. Would that just make his pain worse?

"I'm awake." Like he'd just been taking a nap.

He cracked one eye open. The other one was swollen shut. She did a mental inventory of the rest of his injuries. They'd said there was no internal bleeding, but that was then. Maybe his condition had changed with all the moving they'd done.

"We have to get out of here."

His head shook, a tiny movement. All he could do. "Go."

"I'm not going to leave you here."

"You can get help. Bring them back here for me." But she didn't believe him. It was there in his eyes, that determination to do the right thing. To make sure she was safe. Regardless of what happened to him in the process.

"I'm *not* going to just leave you here."

"You will." He shoved at her with a weak hand. "Go, Ellie. Before they come back."

Someone chuckled. Across the room Deputy Coughlan stepped into view holding a shotgun. Talk about overkill. Then again, he'd had some funny ideas all along.

"I guess I shouldn't be surprised." She turned and sat, her body providing cover for her father's. Whether Coughlan shot her or not, she wasn't going to let the blast hit her father. "Maybe I knew it all along."

He laughed. "Yeah, right."

"Working with Barb. Under a little old lady's thumb this whole time. Figures." She was mad enough she wasn't sure if she could stop herself before she completely provoked him.

He'd probably shoot her then.

Still, all she could consider was how seriously frustrated she was right now. She couldn't help her father. She hadn't been able to help Drew. She hadn't known her best friend was betraying her—along with the rest of the town.

Mad was much better than overcome with sadness. One gave you the strength to do what was necessary, while the other paralyzed you. She had no wish to be overcome with grief. That could come later, when she was alone.

Laney stepped around him. Coughlan's whole demeanor changed. She had a paper in her hand. He paid it no mind, but—wow—the look on his face. He was in love with her and Laney had no idea. She walked over, then frowned back at him. "Lower that shotgun, Peter."

He did.

Under the thumb of another woman? Ellie tried to figure out how she could use that. Meanwhile, Laney pulled a pen from her back pocket and handed it over along with the paper.

"What is this?" The reason why she was still alive?

"Alan wants you to sign this." Laney swallowed. "It's the deed to your father's land, which you will inherit after his death."

"And who am I signing it over to—" She paused. "—in the event of my untimely death?"

Laney paled. "Alan." Her voice broke, but there was no other reaction.

Ellie looked away and shook her head. "No one is going to believe that is legit. I can't deed him property I don't own and have it still be valid...even after my suspicious murder."

"Actually, evidence has come to light." Coughlan took two steps toward her. She saw his boots out the corner of her eyes. "Turns out you're the leader of a group forcing people from their homes. I discovered this, and I came here to confront you. Unfortunately, I had no other choice but to shoot you before you could hurt someone else."

Laney let out a whimper.

But she didn't put up a fight against Coughlan.

Ellie shut her eyes. "You guys have thought of everything, haven't you?" She wanted it to sound sarcastic, as though she still had the strength to put up a fight. But she couldn't, and her words only sounded sad.

"Just sign it."

She looked at her friend. "No."

"He'll kill your father," Laney said. "And then Deputy Coughlan is going to kill you."

"Good luck explaining all that away. Especially when Drew told everything to his friend at the FBI." He trusted

Mark, and Mark was coming here. She prayed the assistant director wouldn't be swayed by easy explanations. That he'd trusted Drew's judgment of her and what was going on in their town.

She prayed justice was done even after they were all killed.

"Ellie."

Outside, a grouping of gunshots sounded. Three round bursts. It was answered by single shots. Someone cried out.

Coughlan ran from the room.

Laney slumped in front of her. "Why couldn't you just do what Franz wanted?"

"Because I'm not going to roll over when a bully comes at me. I stand. And I fight." She lifted to her feet then, just so Laney knew she was prepared to do that right now.

"I tried to tell you. I tried to give you enough information to figure it out," Laney cried. "You and Drew never connected until you went looking for Simon Mills, but when you did that's when I knew you were going to figure it all out. I *wanted* you to. Don't you understand? I basically told you everyone that was in the group. You were too stubborn to realize."

"Like I was too stubborn to realize my best friend was right in the middle of it?"

"I didn't have a choice. And I didn't know what Franz was doing until it was too late to stop it. He's the one that hurts people. Besides, we pay the homeowners plenty of money to go live somewhere else." She sucked in a breath and continued with her emotional excuse.

That's all it was, an excuse.

And Ellie couldn't listen to it right now. She wasn't going to let Laney try and vindicate herself. Not when her father was lying behind her, and Drew was dead. And not just because Franz had decided to go on a rampage just to cover up everything he'd done.

"This has gone too far," she said. "You can't get out of this when you stood there and let him murder Mills."

"He would have shot me, too!"

Ellie shook her head. What was she supposed to say? Laney should have done the right thing from the beginning, and then it would never have reached this point. She couldn't have known it would end with murder. But she should have known it wasn't worth manipulating people just to get her business running. Nothing was worth hurting someone else.

Coughlan ran back in, breathing hard. "Get up." He yelled it as he turned back to the door. "Your boyfriend is here. It's time to go."

She was already standing. Laney grabbed her arm, Ellie wasn't sure why. She couldn't tell if Laney was about to drag her along with her, or if she was standing with Ellie in solidarity.

All she could think of was one thing.

Drew was here.

———

Ellie.

All he could think about was getting to her. His head filled with it. Like it swelled up because his mind was so overwhelmed. Nothing else mattered. Not in the whole world.

Mark went first. Drew followed him down the front walk to the open door, so thankful his friend was here. He needed this backup. And the solidarity of having a friend here to help him.

Mark said, "Where'd he go?"

They'd shot out the front window. Franz had moved out

of sight, but where had he gone? They breached the front door.

"Ellie!" He couldn't hold it back. He had to get to her. Had to know she was okay and that her father was as well. Who cared where Franz went? So long as he didn't—or hadn't—hurt Ellie, Drew knew he would find him. Justice would be done.

A gunshot blasted.

They separated, both moving for opposite walls. Shotgun. Nasty, and Drew had no intention of getting hit by it. Shotguns were serious overkill. Hard to hit what they were aimed at, but they more than made up for it in destruction.

He didn't need a gunshot wound he wouldn't be able to recover from. And neither did he want Mark to get hurt. His friend might be here with authorization from his assistant director. But Drew would have some serious explaining to do if the special agent got hurt here, helping him. Drew didn't want to have to fill out that report. Or face Mark's sister in order to explain what had happened.

He fired twice and then moved to the living room for cover. Looked around for Franz. There was a closet, but nowhere else the man could have been hiding. There was no furniture at all. So he had to have headed for the kitchen.

"Drew!" Her voice rang down the hall.

The shotgun ratcheted, and then he fired again.

Everything in Drew wanted to rush forward, down the hall. Get to Ellie.

Between them, one of Franz's guys—or the man himself —stood with a loaded shotgun. Behind cover. Hiding somewhere Drew couldn't see.

He heard the guy ready it to fire again. Franz hadn't had a shotgun when he'd been in the front window. Was this someone else?

Drew motioned to Mark with a tip of his head, then

disappeared. Hopefully this open plan layout meant there was a way from the living room to the kitchen, then to the hallway where that gunman stood. Could he cut the guy off? Come up on him from another direction and take him down?

He prayed again, not having stopped since all this kicked off. Just one long, continuous dialogue. And wasn't that the way it was supposed to be? Too bad it took Ellie being in mortal danger to get him to figure out how that worked. He couldn't just pray whenever he remembered. He needed to keep that dialogue going all the time.

Sorry, Lord. Drew was going to keep asking for help, though. They all needed it.

He reached the kitchen and found the back door open. He rushed to it, finding cover. Franz raced down the hill behind the house. Dirt, no landscaping yet, and it was slippery. He stumbled. Drew could follow his footprints. But not until he got that gunman neutralized.

Mark fired off two shots from his SIG, still in the front hallway.

The shotgun-wielding man fired back.

Drew crept to the refrigerator, not plugged in yet, and leaned his shoulder against it. He looked around the corner.

Deputy Coughlan.

Behind him was a room, but Drew couldn't see inside. And if he called out again he would give away his position. Never mind that he'd find out where Ellie was. She was here, and his heart cared more about that. Enough to try and convince his brain that calling out and giving himself away was the thing to do.

Drew pushed all of it aside and lifted his weapon. "Put it down, Coughlan. It's over."

The deputy swung around, rage on his face. Drew had never liked that guy. And he certainly didn't trust him.

Drew launched his body away from the spot where he'd been standing. The shotgun blast filled the air with cordite and the sound of a firework. Drew hit the floor, his ears ringing. He lifted his gun and put pressure on the trigger.

A gun went off, but not his.

Coughlan fell to the ground, clutching his shoulder.

"Hold your fire!" Ellie stepped out of the room. She kicked the shotgun away from Coughlan. Saw Mark.

Turned.

Then she saw him, standing there staring back at her. Her jaw dropped. "It's really you. I thought I was imagining it."

Mark came over, sliding his SIG back into its holster. "One for me?"

Drew got up. "Both of them." He motioned to where Laney stood.

"I'll do it." Ellie held out her hands. Mark handed her a pair of handcuffs. Drew had another pair, which Mark used to secure Coughlan while he lay on the floor moaning. Bleeding. The man had a gunshot in his shoulder, but they didn't want him pulling anything before they got him to the hospital under armed guard. He looked fit and able to try something. Like go for someone's weapon.

There was still the matter of the emergency alert. It needed to be called back. Things had to go back to normal at some point. Hopefully soon. But there was one more thing they had to do before they could tell everyone it was safe to come out of their homes.

"Franz is out there. I need to go after him." If they waited much longer, the guy was going to get away. Drew turned to Laney, now wearing cuffs courtesy of her former best friend. "Where would he go?"

Franz was on the run—probably split when he'd seen the FBI agent show up. He would likely grab a stash of personal belongings and cash, and then he'd be in the wind. They couldn't let that happen.

Laney sniffed. "He has an office." She lifted both hands and pointed west. "At the other end of the neighborhood. It's a trailer."

Drew glanced at Mark. He was staring at Laney with an interesting expression on his face. "Mark."

His friend blinked, then looked at him.

"Both of these people need to be in custody."

Ellie said, "Pending a list of serious charges." She looked about as happy as he felt.

Drew pushed out a breath. "You got this?"

Mark nodded. "Go get that other guy. I'll call this in."

"State police?" Ellie asked him.

Mark nodded. "I have them on their way. They're completely up to speed on what's happening. At least, they were before we came into this house."

Ellie said, "Okay. Good." Then she turned to him. "Let's go get Franz."

"You're coming with me?"

She said, "Are you going?"

He nodded. Of course he was. There was no way he'd let a murderer get away. Who knew what Franz could tell him about his father's death? The man might be a criminal and was probably a liar along with it, but Drew wanted the chance to find out anything he could.

"Then yes, I'm coming." Ellie lifted her chin. "You think I'm going to let you do it alone?"

Drew said, "No, ma'am."

Mark coughed to cover his laugh. Drew didn't much care. He pulled the second gun from his belt and handed it to her. At the back door, he said, "Ellie." Just loud enough to get her attention.

She turned to him.

Drew leaned down and pressed his lips to hers. "I'm glad you're okay."

She touched both sides of his face, awkward with a gun in one hand. Then she tugged his head down and kissed him far more thoroughly than he'd kissed her. When she was done, he lifted his head, a smile playing on his lips.

She said, "You, too."

And then they went to find Franz.

Together.

20

The patio stopped around eight feet from the back door. Beyond that was nothing but dirt.

"We could head around front. Get the truck," Drew said. "Drive over there."

She shook her head and headed out. "He'll hear us coming."

"Barb didn't."

Did he have an answer for everything? They'd been enjoying a very nice—but also distracting—kiss just a moment ago. Now they were at odds again.

"This way." He motioned to the dirt ahead of him, angling west.

She was just looking for the road on the other side of this hill. Still, she followed him. Then she saw it. Footprints in the dirt. "He came this way?"

"I saw him run."

"You didn't go after him?" She realized how that sounded the second the words left her lips. "Never mind. I'd have done the rescue part first as well."

"Good," he said, over his shoulder to where she followed

him. "Because I was worried for a second you'd have left me there."

"You're a big strong guy, you'd have been able to handle it."

"So could you," he said. "And I know that because you *did*. You got yourself and your father through it, long enough for me to show up with Mark."

Her father. Seeing Drew, her relief had been so all encompassing that she had forgotten for a second her father was back in that room. "I'm still praying he comes out of this still in one piece."

"They hurt him?"

She didn't have an answer. "I just hope he's okay when Mark gets him back to the hospital."

Drew hit a concrete sidewalk and pushed himself onward with a groan. Like his jog wanted to be a sprint, but he just couldn't make his body move any faster. He led the way to the far end of the deserted neighborhood where the office was. The pace was punishing. The only way she knew he felt it as well was because of the heavy breaths he heaved out each time.

Ellie was about ready to collapse. But the idea they could be seconds away from bringing down a murderer injected energy into muscle and sinew. She prayed for the strength to go beyond her considerable limits right now. God could gift her with energy and focus.

She needed it desperately.

She needed Him.

And yet, for years she'd pushed God away. She'd refused to let Him come in, afraid that comfort would mean weakness. She'd preferred to shut herself off from any feelings, good or bad. Loss was something she would carry with her for the rest of her life. But hopefully she could share that with Drew, and a renewed relationship with her Heavenly Father. A relationship full of rich blessings.

She prayed that Drew was the beginning of a lifetime of blessings.

"There!"

She saw it as well. The trailer that housed the office for this neighborhood under construction. The light inside was on, and the front door was open. "He's in there."

Energy surged through her. They were so close to finishing this she could almost taste it.

Drew slowed. He held out his arm, and she allowed him to sweep her to one side. It wouldn't go well if they alerted Franz to the fact they were outside. They angled to the right of the door.

Inside she heard something hit the floor and smash. A computer monitor maybe? Did he know breaking it didn't destroy the hard drive? Unless it was one of those built-in computers.

She looked at Drew and saw his teeth set hard, the muscle in his jaw tense enough it stood out.

Liquid spilled, and the sound continued. A pour of whatever it was out onto the floor. The furniture. She smelled it. "Gasoline."

He had to have grabbed it from some generator, or other equipment. A contractor's extra stash for when his motor ran out.

And now he was using it to burn down the office.

Drew said, "You take the back. Make sure you grab him if he comes out. I'll watch the front."

The pouring stopped. He wasn't going to go in, but would wait for Alan to come out.

She nodded, then raced around to the rear door around back. She watched the windows and saw when the flicker of flames began. Heard the whoosh as gasoline caught fire, ignited to burn. Consuming everything.

Did Alan Franz plan to die inside?

She shifted her weight, ready to move whichever direction was necessary. Held her gun loose in front of her. Ready to shoot at—

The back door flung open, and Alan Franz stumbled out, coughing. Smoke poured out along with him. Not a firebug, he seemed surprised and…kind of charred.

"Hands!"

He started.

"Put them up, Franz. You're under arrest!"

His face twisted into a grimace.

"Down on the ground. On your knees."

She saw him hesitate, but she had him. He lowered to kneel on the dirt. She kept her attention on the whole scene. Everything around her, and not just the man and the fire and herself. Drew had been surprised when that man hit him at the bowling alley. She wasn't going to allow the same thing to happen to her.

"Drew!" She called for him, then said to Franz, "Interlock your fingers behind your head." When her partner rounded the single-wide office, she said, "I need cover."

He nodded. "On it." He kept his gun aimed at Alan.

She stowed her weapon in the holster on her hip and walked around Drew, careful not to move between his gun and the bank manager. She pulled a zip tie from her partner's back pocket and used it to secure Alan's hands. "I need some of these. They're pretty handy." She hauled Alan to his feet.

"Alan Franz, you have the right to remain silent." The rest of the Miranda rights rolled off her tongue.

Alan started to shake his head before she'd even finished

outlining his rights as she had explained them to him. "No one's going to point a finger at me. You have nothing."

"Yeah," she said, sighing. "Except for the fact we witnessed you shoot Simon Mills. Aside from that, nothing. Right, Drew?"

His lips twitched.

Alan shifted, turning his shoulders to get a look at her face.

She wasn't that interested in any kind of explanation. Or excuse. "Let's go."

They set off, back toward the house where he'd held her hostage. "Laney was the one who said you wanted me to sign over my father's property. To sell it to you. Before you *killed me.* You think I'm going to believe that was all some kind of lie?"

"It's true." Alan didn't seem quite so scary now that he was in her custody. She'd seen him shoot someone, but he wasn't going to hurt anyone else. Not now.

He continued, "I was forced to do it. You don't know what he's like. We're all under his thumb."

Drew put out a hand, forcing them both to stop. He moved so his face was close to Alan's. "Are you saying someone else is in charge of this little group of yours?"

Alan shifted. To be fair, he seemed a little nervous.

Drew said, "You're scared."

Alan nodded, a jerky movement.

"You just burned down that trailer to save your own skin," Ellie said. "And now we're supposed to believe you're being forced to do all this?" She'd seen absolutely no sign so far that he was taking orders from someone else. "Why don't you tell us who it is?"

"No." He shook his head. "I'll be dead before I'm booked into the county jail. I'm not saying anything."

ELLIE HAD SEEN her father off in an ambulance, promising she would be there as soon as she wrapped up this scene. Drew was glad for that. He was feeling selfish, not wanting to let her out of his sight. Even to see her father? His emotions were all over the place.

He was completely exhausted, but he also wanted to scoop her up in his arms, pile her in a car and take her somewhere quiet where they could eat something and get some rest. Maybe watch a movie neither of them cared about and fall asleep at opposite ends of a couch.

All of which was ridiculous, considering they hadn't established any kind of relationship.

Yet.

"Dude."

He spun to face his friend, jarred from his thoughts. "Don't call me that."

"You weren't responding to anything else. Are you asleep on your feet?"

"Probably."

"And your knee?" Mark asked.

"If I sit down, I doubt I'll be able to get up again."

"What? You won't?" Ellie closed the rest of the distance between them, breaking off the conversation she'd been having with two officers of the state police. "I thought you were doing all right."

Drew wasn't going to lie to her.

Mark rocked back on his heels, a smile on his face. "The stoic hero wishes to plead the fifth on the subject of how badly he hurts right now."

Drew could have punched his friend. Thankfully, though, Ellie laughed. Then she clapped her hands over her mouth. "Sorry. That's not funny."

Drew shook his head. "It's not *not* funny."

"Yeah." She sobered. "Like Alan telling us there's someone else at the head of the class."

He nodded. They had Laney, Deputy Coughlan, and Alan all in custody. Surely one of the three could tell them who was in charge. If there even *was* someone in charge.

"You think he was telling the truth?" Mark asked the question, half turned to observe the state police vehicles where they'd stashed the three separately so they couldn't talk to each other.

Drew wasn't sure. But he didn't have the chance to say anything because the state police captain strode over, his hand out. "Drew Turner. It's good to meet you. Heard a lot."

"You too, Captain…?"

"Peakes." He motioned to Mark. "Your friend here keeps us apprised on your uh…*activities* for the bureau."

Drew grinned. So he was the subject of stories Mark told to his cop buddies. He folded his arms and glanced aside at his friend. "Is that right?"

Mark shook his head. "We need to talk to all three, and we have to do it simultaneously. We need answers now. There isn't time to play them off against each other."

Ellie, who'd been glancing curiously between them all with a seriously cute look on her face, said, "We can convince them that if they're the first to talk, they'll get the lightest consequences."

Captain Peakes said, "What's your read on them, Deputy Maxwell? Which do you think will be the easiest to get talking?"

One was her colleague. One was the bank manager and a murderer.

The other was supposed to be her best friend.

Ellie said, "Laney."

He'd known that was what she would say before she even

said it. Ellie was going to put aside her hurt and do her job, just like she had been doing for years. But it worked. He knew she felt, and did so deeply. Though he figured she didn't want to admit to that.

"I'll go with you."

She turned to him. Drew said, "Mark can take the deputy, pressure him as a federal agent. The captain and his people can take Alan Franz. That leaves us with Laney." He saw the question on her face, and answered it. This wasn't about him babysitting her or thinking she couldn't do her job. "I can't question anyone. I'm not a cop, so I don't have that authority."

This wasn't about him taking over. It was about him supporting her.

"Okay." Agreement, but it was all professional. Nothing more.

The others agreed, so he and Ellie went to the vehicle where Laney sat looking out the window at them.

They both rounded the car. Ellie got in the back while Drew got in the driver's seat.

"Don't bother." Laney's voice was quiet, and sad.

"Too bad," Ellie said. "You don't have a choice now. Like you're not going to have a choice when they convict you and send you to jail. How long that sentence is will be entirely up to you, and what you say in this car right now."

Drew turned to see Laney frown. He'd pulled out his phone and was recording the conversation, so they could admit it as evidence of her cooperation—or her guilt.

"What are you talking about?" She glanced between them, her gaze not quite landing on her best friend. Like it was too painful to face Ellie. Drew understood that. She was worried she'd ruined the trust between them, and to be honest she had.

Would they be able to repair it?

Drew said, "When we were talking to Alan Franz, he mentioned someone else. He told us that person is the one pulling all the strings. That they are the one in charge, and he was just following orders."

Laney's lips thinned.

Ellie said, "Do you know who that person is, Lane?" Did she know she'd dropped the "y" in her friend's name like that? The way two people who cared about each other would do. The way her father had called her "El."

Laney looked out the window again. "Is that what they're asking them?"

Ellie said, "Yes. And if you're first to cooperate, that's going to look good with the judge."

"Are you going to visit me in jail?"

"If that's what you want."

Laney turned back from the window. "I do. I want us to work our way back to friendship."

"That's gonna take some time," Ellie said. "But I want to try."

Drew swelled with pride. This woman's strengths knew uncharted depths, so deep he wondered if even she was aware of how far down it went. That she could draw on it like this, not with ease but with the strength of her resolve.

She looked like she was about to cry, so Drew broke off his gaze. He didn't want to trigger that well of emotion she was fighting to keep in check.

Later there would be plenty of time for her to cry on his shoulder. To take her to her father, so she could cry on his. Drew wanted dinners. Coffee dates. He wanted her to come on an assignment with him over a few days of vacation, just because he knew how much her strengths would mean to his work. And he was pretty sure he could persuade Mark that it was a good idea.

Or he would give up the work that took him out of town. Stay local and take pictures for a living.

"Alan Franz did a lot because he wanted to, but there was someone giving orders."

When she didn't say more, Drew said, "Who?"

Laney sucked in a breath, then said, "Mayor Porter." She lifted her gaze to meet his and said, "He's the one who killed your father."

21

The hallway was dark except for a security light at the far end. His door open, slightly ajar. Not enough to see the man inside.

She unsnapped the strap that secured her gun in its holster. Ellie left it where it was, her thumb in the pocket of her jeans so it was close enough. But she'd still look casual.

Was she really going to do this?

Everything that had happened the past few days was because she'd sought out a man. The first time, she'd gone to Drew for help. Professional assistance from someone she'd thought was a private investigator. Now she knew he was far more than that.

Her favorite artist.

A federal contractor.

There was so much to him that she had no doubt she'd be discovering new sides for years to come. Ellie was very much looking forward to it.

She prayed as she approached the door. Her body had been pushed to the limit, and this wasn't done. It would be soon, but right now she needed to be at her best. Focused.

Her reactions on point. If he had a weapon, Ellie might be forced to make that split second decision no cop wanted to make. Fatigue could cost her the future she wanted with Drew.

Ellie listened for any sound from the inside of the office. Then she toed the door open.

He sat at his desk, the light from the desk lamp a yellow glow that illuminated his face but left swaths of dark shadows that twisted his features.

"Mr. Mayor."

He let out a long sigh. "Deputy Maxwell."

She hadn't voted for him. She'd voted for the other candidate, a woman. Mayor Porter had worked in this office for far too long. With that power had come a sense of entitlement and the desire to subvert people's will in order to further his own gain.

She stepped inside, barely over the threshold. The movement shifted the wire and tugged on the tape she'd secured high on her front, underneath the open collar of her sheriff's department uniform.

"It's time to go, Mayor Porter. It's over."

She wasn't much concerned with the need to get him to confess. Although people often tended to say in the dark what they would never say in the light. She'd much rather just secure him in the cuffs she had on the back of her belt and walk him outside. To where the state police kept watch out of courtesy to her—and her request to make this approach alone.

To where Drew paced as he waited for her to come out.

He didn't move except to turn his head and stare out the window, his view of the town. All that was visible from this lofty position.

"Porter."

He needed to get up and move around his desk. That was the best scenario.

There were several possible outcomes, and Ellie was rooting for the one that called for none of their blood spilled on the carpet.

"I'm glad it's you."

Ellie forced herself not to react. Anything she said or did might set off a chain reaction, and he could have a weapon over there.

He kept staring out the window. "Don't you want to know why?"

"I want you to come over here with your hands on your head."

"So like your father."

"He covered for you." She didn't want to say even that, not with the state police listening. But she couldn't let that lie.

Porter sighed, a slight shake of his head. "We do what we must. A legacy handed down, imprinted on our DNA. It's what built this town."

"You had a choice. You didn't have to destroy people's lives." And she hadn't even gotten to the murders yet.

She wanted to cry, "Why?" but what would that solve? Whatever his answer, it wasn't going to make her feel better. Nothing was going to repair the damage of what he'd done. Too many people's lives established in this town had been destroyed. They'd wanted to live here, and they'd been forced to leave.

"It got out of control."

"You think?" She lifted the hand opposite her gun side, and then let it fall back down. "People are dead, Mr. Mayor. And someone has to answer for that."

He glanced at her.

"Walk over here slowly. Now." She raised her voice

slightly, and it rang with authority. "Hands where I can see them."

"I suppose it's for the best." He pushed the chair up and stood.

"It's what happens when all the wrong you've done finally catches up with you. Like murdering Drew's father."

It slipped out. Ellie gritted her back teeth together. She shouldn't have said that. Now wasn't the time to get into it. He needed to be walking over here so she could arrest him, but she was just so seriously frustrated she wanted to punch a hole in the wall.

"I've done so many things. You choose to condemn me for that?"

"I would choose to condemn you for all of it, every single thing you've done, but it's not up to me. It's up to the law."

He sighed. "Always so high and mighty, you Maxwells. Like you're above everyone else."

"A murderer? Yeah, maybe." She bit back what else she wanted to say, choosing instead to try and make peace. "But I'm not perfect. Far from it."

She wandered to him with measured steps. "Let's go, Porter." She sounded as tired as she was. Too tired to stand here while he explained everything to her, when she was pretty sure most of it she didn't want to know.

"I was going to make this town great." He held his hands out, palms empty. "Too many naysayers. People don't want better, even if you hand it to them on a platter. Condo developments, shopping centers. Big city. Small town. They want two different lives and complain about both, whichever way you give it to them."

She grabbed one hand and twisted it behind him, then the other. She secured both in a pair of cuffs. "So your response is to murder people?"

"Jedidiah Turner was a liability. Just like the rest of them.

Too much mouth, too willing to give up what good I could provide."

"So he wanted to tell someone what you were doing? Like Natalie Benson, the real estate office receptionist?"

"Tired of leaning on people. Jed didn't want to make any more threats."

He wasn't going to admit to killing Natalie? Had it been Alan Franz?

She walked the mayor to the door of his office and down the hallway. "He was an enforcer for you?"

"We all have skills. His were breaking legs and getting people to cooperate." The mayor's steps stuttered as he spotted Drew at the end of the hallway. "Your father wasn't a good man."

Drew said nothing.

"It was just business."

"And the land you've done nothing with?" She walked the mayor past him. "The cabin is still there, lying in ruins."

"Just business."

Ellie handed the mayor over to the state police captain. With the sheriff's department currently in a shambles, there was no way they could root out how far this corruption had spread. Their office was compromised. Who knew how long it would take to set everything to rights? Make sure they had all the players in custody.

She watched from the steps of city hall as they loaded the mayor into the back of one of their vehicles and drove him away to be booked into custody. Prosecuted. It was a small measure of comfort but nothing could repair the damage these people had done.

She of all people knew the cost of destruction like that. The only way forward was one step at a time. One prayer at a time.

Drew moved to stand beside her, laying a hand on the

back of her neck. He gave her a small squeeze. Solidarity. Affection.

In a matter of days, her life had shifted in a way that would never again be the same. But she never wanted it to be the same ever again. Ellie understood the importance of the love from the people in her life.

Of being open. Cared for.

"Can we go see my dad?"

———

Likely that was all the answer Drew was going to get from the mayor. He didn't want to go digging into his father's past. Into the life of a man he hadn't liked at all. Sure, at the time he had tried to love him, simply because he was his father. But he and his father didn't have a connection at all. His father hadn't known what true fatherhood was.

Eric had shown him. Loved him, appreciated him. Taken him in and cared for him. Shown him how to be a gentleman. To channel his emotions when they got out of control.

So many ways.

Drew had much to be thankful for. Maybe he should express his gratitude in person, and maybe Ellie would want to go with him.

He tugged on her arm just before she stepped inside the hospital room where her dad had been admitted.

"What?"

I love you. No, wait. That would be weird. It was way too soon. "Wanna go to Florida with me?"

Her mouth opened. Closed. She said, "Do you know what? I'm not sure I've taken a vacation in *years*."

"Guess you're due, then."

A gleam flashed in her tired eyes. "Guess I am."

She didn't move. He waited, seeing what would come

next. He was guessing it would be good. After the past few days, they were certainly due for an abundance of goodness.

Then Ellie reached up. She touched the sides of his face. "Is it weird that I think I might be in love with you?"

"Not at all." His throat clogged. Drew slid his arms around her waist and gathered her close.

She tipped up onto the balls of her feet and touched her lips to his. Beyond her, he spotted movement. He tensed, before he realized it was Mark.

He gave her a squeeze. "Go check on your dad."

She glanced back over her shoulder, then at him. With one more soft touch of her lips to his, she disappeared into her dad's room.

Mark strode over, a mischievous smile curling his lips. "What?"

"Some woman you've got there," he said. "I'm thinking your life will not be boring."

"I'm going to take her to see Eric and Alma."

"Meeting the parents? Already?"

Drew shrugged. "Ellie and I might not have known each other for years, but we've been a part of each other's lives for quite awhile."

"History." A dark look washed over Mark's face.

"What's that about?"

Mark shook his head. "Nothing. Just a long story. I'll tell you sometime."

"I'd like to hear it."

If the last few days had taught him anything, it was that he needed to stop living on the outside of his own life. Ellie had crossed his path in a way he couldn't deny. She'd forced him to face the fact he didn't trust other people with himself. Now that they'd begun the process of building something, he could appreciate the power of being known. He trusted her.

Trusted what she saw in him. That he was safe to give his feelings to her.

The same way she was safe with him.

He turned to Mark. "Tell the director that I want out."

"Out?"

"I'm not available now. I need to be here."

"She have anything to do with that?" He motioned to the closed door.

Drew shrugged. "Time to refocus. I've got a house to rebuild, a horse to find. Then I'll be starting a new journey."

He would need to be in town on a permanent basis if he was going to persuade Ellie she should run for sheriff.

"Can't say I'm happy about that. But I am happy *for* you." He held out his hand. "It's been a pleasure."

Drew shook his friend's hand. "Liar."

Mark barked out a laugh. "Maybe. Guess you'll never know."

"Thanks for coming to help. Sorry about Alvarez."

Mark said, "Apparently he got shot a few weeks ago." He made a face. "Didn't tell me that. Recovery will be slow, but he'll get back up to speed soon enough."

Drew nodded. "Tell him I appreciate his help." He held out his hand. "And yours."

"So you said." Mark shook his hand. "Until next time?"

"Sure." He watched his friend wander away and then let himself into Will's room. The former sheriff was laid up, eyes closed. Ellie had his hand in hers.

Drew took in the scene, for once not feeling the grief for something he would never know. His life was rich. He would rather have realized that without their lives being in danger, but it had been necessary to uncover the poison that had spread beneath the surface of the town.

The players were all behind bars. Justice would be done.

The rest of the residents could breathe easy, knowing they were safe.

Drew wanted to stick around town so he could help. Support Ellie. See how he could pitch in and make sure their town was turned around. Brought back to the good he knew was possible. Because he could see it in her when she looked at him.

Ellie carved out a safe place he could be himself. In return, he was going to fan that flame of life he saw flickering in her eyes. He was going to do everything he could to make her life the best it could possibly be. Because she deserved nothing less than happiness. Enjoyment of all the ways God had blessed them.

He had given them each other.

She walked over. "What are you thinking?"

"Other than we both need to crash?"

"It's not that."

She was right. That wasn't what he'd been thinking, but it was what both of them needed right now. Time to rest. To heal.

He needed to rebuild Eric and Alma's house.

"That I'm happy, and I can't remember really feeling that before." She opened her mouth to say something, but there was more he needed to get out. "And I'm glad it's you. That brown-eyed girl with the ponytail. The one who looked at me like I turned the world, just by getting out of bed in the morning."

She gasped. "You remember?"

"You were wearing a pink T-shirt." In his mind, he could still see the look on her face. Walking down the hall of their high school. Not much had been good about his life back then. When it did come he'd soaked up every drop of it, like a man lost in the desert.

Because that was what his life had been.

Now she filled those dry places in him. Bringing rain.

"I remember that shirt." She winced. "I'd borrowed it from Laney because I spilled chocolate milk on my shirt at lunch, and she always packed an extra one just in case."

She was babbling. Nervous, because of what he'd thought about her years ago in the hallway at school? "It was cute." He smiled. "You were cute."

"Maybe."

"You still are." Some things had changed, but not that. Not the most important stuff. The things that made up who they were. Despite the years. Despite the pain they'd both gone through. In the end, God had made them who they were.

A perfect match for each other.

She said, "Fine, but don't tell anyone. If it gets out, me and that pink shirt, it'll ruin my cop reputation."

He smiled and touched his lips to hers. "It'll be our secret."

EPILOGUE

One year later

"I now pronounce you husband and wife."

Drew didn't need to wait for any invitation to pull Ellie close for a kiss. The small gathering of friends and family cheered. The cool Florida winter air blew a light breeze that lifted strands of her curled hair, touching them to where their lips met.

He pulled back, seeing nothing but her. "I love you, Sheriff Maxwell."

She smiled. Truth was, she hadn't stopped smiling since she walked down the aisle in bare feet, her arm linked with her father's.

Drew's toes curled into the sand.

The past year had been one of the longest of his life. Ellie had won her bid for sheriff. During a time when he'd been staking a claim of his own—the one on her heart.

And she did have his heart. He felt it in every touch and heard it in every word she said to him.

Especially when he'd given her that early wedding

present. Her favorite photo to hang on the wall in her office. He'd also bought her a horse of her own that he was going to give her when they got home.

"I love you too." Her smile got even wider. "Mayor North."

She'd convinced him. Drew had been skeptical at first, but he'd quickly realized the good he could do as the town mayor. Putting things to rights. Building a better town, one that welcomed people instead of forcing them away. Once the whole scheme came out, people had looked at him differently. He'd been able to forge a new reputation.

"Ready?" He held out his hand, eager to greet their life together.

She slipped her hand into his. "Always."

ALSO BY LISA PHILLIPS

Northwest Counter Terrorism Taskforce series:

First Wave - Book 1

Second Chance - Book 2

Third Hour - Book 3

Fourth Day - Book 4

Final Stand - Book 5

Find out more HERE

Or, buy the complete series at a discounted rate!

Northwest Counter Terrorism Box Set

Learn more about Lisa's small town series, Last Chance County. Home of several book series, including: Last Chance County, Last Chance Fire & Rescue and Chevalier Protection Specialists.

The Last Chance County saga begins with Expired Refuge, which you can find here: books2read.com/ExpiredRefuge .

Find out about Lisa's other books on her website:

https://authorlisaphillips.com

ABOUT THE AUTHOR

Find out more about Lisa Phillips at her website, where you can check out her work with Sunrise Publishing and find Lisa on Social Media.
https://authorlisaphillips.com/about-the-author

If you loved this book, please consider sharing about it on social media. Or leave a review at your book retailer website, on Goodreads, or on Bookbub. Your review will help others find great books to entertain and encourage them! For a FREE novel from Lisa Phillips, check out the link below to connect to Lisa's newsletter and be the first to hear about sales, new books, and recommendations for your TBR pile.

https://authorlisaphillips.com/subscribe

facebook.com/authorlisaphillips
instagram.com/lisaphillipsbks
bookbub.com/authors/lisa-phillips